a
Dark Eart[
novel

A Dark and Rising Tide

Debra Castaneda

SHADOW
CANYON
— *press* —

ISBN: 979-8-9877469-6-7
Edited by: Lyndsey Smith, Horrorsmith Editing
Cover design by: James, GoOnWrite.com

To Jim
I can't imagine doing this without you.

Chapter 1

overcast
53°

If the man in the small boat didn't sit down, it would tip over.

He had no business being out there—a tourist probably getting his first glimpse of a great white shark circling just below the surface. A storm was coming, and Marty, the owner of Boat & Tackle, should have closed shop. But he liked money as much as he did the whiskey in his stainless steel coffee mug, and he obviously thought he could sneak in a few rentals before calling it a day.

Marty never seemed to learn his lesson, renting his motorized skiffs to anyone over twenty-one with a credit card, including men who'd knocked back too many beermosas in the restaurant at the end of the pier.

Carla scowled and wiped at a stubborn window smudge. The entire back of the restaurant was one plate of glass after another, and she had a clear shot of the action. Marty was hanging over the railing, shouting instructions and probably confusing the hell out of the boater. A small group of onlookers peered over the railing.

Sliding open the glass door, Carla stepped outside on the deck, still clutching the damp rag. The relentless winter surf roared two dozen yards away—a distance that didn't seem nearly far enough during high tide. The damp air was chilly and heavy with the scent of the sea. Cries of seagulls overhead pierced through the rumble of crashing waves.

Carla had weathered many storms since she'd taken over Pancha's Mexican Restaurant from her parents twelve years ago, and she knew the forecasts were often wrong. She remembered the last time meteorologists had predicted a massive storm. Everyone had panicked and evacuated, but the storm had gone off course. Carla closed the restaurant for nothing and had paid to stay in a motel, with no money coming in.

This time, no matter how dire the forecasts, she was determined not to leave. Besides, her apartment was on the second floor. Even if Ocean View Drive flooded, she'd be safe up there.

The small red boat reached the base of the stairs below the pier. Marty was down there, trying to help the man out.

"They're both going to end up in the water."

Carla glanced over in surprise. It was Matt Harmon, her best friend's husband and owner of the fish restaurant next door.

"I thought you decided not to open today."

He pulled a face. "Yuki reminded me we booked a private party for lunch. A bunch of women coming from Stockton or someplace for a bridal shower."

"I guess they haven't been watching the news," Carla said, one eye still on the men stumbling up the ramp.

Matt scraped a hand through what was left of his red hair. "I just hope they have a designated driver. The last shower we had got pretty wild."

"I remember. They came to my place afterwards, and one of them threw up nachos. That shit ended up on the ceiling."

Matt grimaced. "Yuki told me. Sorry." He jerked his head in the direction of the pier. "Think that dude out there got bumped by a shark?"

Carla laughed. "Maybe he just lost his phone."

The smile quickly vanished. A blank look spread over her face as she recalled her son's panic when his phone fell into the creek while they were kayaking together.

Days later, she'd lost him.

Her throat tightened.

Breathe. Just breathe. Like the therapist said.

Matt swiveled to face her. "You okay?"

As okay as I'll ever be. She didn't need to tell Matt that. He knew. Knew all about it. Most people did, even if they didn't say anything.

Inside, the phone rang. Carla wished Matt good luck with the bridal shower lunch, then ran in to answer it. It was an old-fashioned land line, an ugly beige box stuck to the wall next to the bar, with a long cord that tended to tangle. She only kept it because some of the locals still used it, and they constituted most of her clientele during the off-season.

"You're probably wondering what the hell is going on over here," Sue said without preamble. Carla had known the woman since her parents opened the restaurant forty years ago. Sue was the sensible half of Boat & Tackle.

"The guy on the boat saw a shark?" Carla guessed.

"No, no sharks. Said he was fishing, caught something, and was pulling it in, but when he saw what it was, it scared the bejeesus out of him, and he couldn't figure out how to get it off the line, so he dropped the darn rod. It was one of our nicer rentals, of course."

Carla nudged open the swinging door into the kitchen and peered through the gap. Gilbert was dropping sprigs of cilantro into a steel pot bubbling on the stove. The skull tattoos on his arms were so old, the lines had grown blurry, and they now looked like green blobs against his brown skin.

In the distance, a siren wailed.

"You called an ambulance?" The man appeared to have made it off the skiff just fine.

"We did," Sue said, voice rising with excitement. "Whatever it was, stung him. Real bad."

"A jellyfish?"

"Nope. Said it was big and ugly and got him with the end of a long tentacle or something."

Carla frowned. She was no expert on fish, but she'd never heard of anything like that in the Monterey Bay.

"Did you call Amalia?"

Amalia owned San Refugio Charters, Whale Watching & Cruises. She ran her business out of an office on the other side of the fish restaurant, next to the swollen creek. Amalia could name most of the species out there.

"Yup. She's coming over now, as a matter of fact." Sue paused. "You should see the guy's arm where it got him. It's got a hole in it, and it's all purple and gross-looking, and he's acting real out of it. I hope he doesn't have a fit or something before the paramedics get here."

The wailing siren drew closer.

"That's terrible," Carla muttered. If the restaurant weren't opening soon, she'd run over there and look for herself.

"I tried calling Peter, but he didn't answer," Sue said, sounding offended.

Peter was a former park ranger and state lifeguard. He lived in the San Refugio Ocean Condominiums, the unit closest to the water. On many a night, Carla helped keep his bed warm and, in the morning, cooked chilaquiles in a tiny kitchen with chipped turquoise tiles. The place had to be worth two million dollars.

"Peter went to the East Bay to see his nephews," she explained.

"He's a good guy. You should make him put a ring on it."

Sue hung up before Carla could think of a snappy comeback.

Carla went out on the deck, just in time to see the paramedics and an ambulance roll past the condos, red lights flashing.

She watched the vehicles make their way toward the far end of the rickety pier. It was a miracle the thing was still standing. In her four decades in the seaside village, several storms had come through and done their best to knock it down, but it still stood.

Her gaze drifted to the sea. The sky was darkening—gray clouds rolling over the bay.

The bay where her only child rested in a watery grave.

Chapter 2

breezy

Peter listened to the all-news radio station on the long drive back to San Refugio. By the time he hit Highway 17, the storm had been upgraded to a bomb cyclone and was now expected to hit late Friday or early Saturday.

The last atmospheric river to aim its hose at San Refugio had flooded the entire village.

"Damn." He winced.

The storm couldn't have come at a worse time. He'd pulled a muscle roughhousing with his nephews, and his lower back hurt like hell. The windows at his condo needed boarding up for the storm, and he'd have to build a barrier of sandbags to divert water from the doors. His back was in no condition to accomplish either task.

Peter cautiously navigated his truck around the potholes to avoid jostling his spine while heading downhill. As he got closer to San Refugio, he noticed tractors working their way along the beach, fortifying the sand berm.

The city was taking the bomb cyclone forecast seriously.

Not that a ridge of sand would be enough to hold back the storm's power. At best, in the event of a tidal surge, the berm might buy some time for the businesses along Ocean View Drive, but it would do nothing for the San Refugio Ocean Condos.

He rounded a bend, and Fickle Point came into view.

Surfers crowded the water, taking advantage of the large swells created by the impending weather. A bicycle whizzed past, ridden by a lean figure in a wet suit, a banana-yellow surfboard in a side-mounted rack. Peter'd know that surfboard anywhere. It belonged to Quint, a local firefighter fresh off his shift.

At the Hotel & Suites, Peter made a sharp right, drove to the end of the short road leading to the pier, and swiped a magnetic card on the reader. The electronic arm lifted, and he pulled his truck into his reserved space.

He grabbed his backpack and looked over at the water. A chain was strung across the old wooden walkway. A laminated sign taped to a red plastic sawhorse read: PIER CLOSED. DO NOT GO BEYOND THIS POINT.

Of the ten vintage homes in the San Refugio Ocean Condos, only half had full-time residents. The others were used as vacation homes. Short-term rentals weren't allowed. The buildings had thick adobe walls painted cream, trimmed in dark brown, with red tile roofs. They were the oldest condos in the state, built decades before building codes prohibited construction so close to the ocean.

Peter walked down the narrow sidewalk separating the condos from Cortina Creek. The unit next to his was owned by out-of-towners and overseen by a local property management company. The windows were already boarded up. The creek on the other side of the wall eventually curved left, replaced by sand that stretched to the crashing surf.

Maggie Spenger was outside her place three doors down, sitting on a green plastic patio chair and drinking a glass of white wine. She had to be pushing seventy-five. Maggie had been friends with Peter's mother, so he'd known her since his folks bought the place in 1983. Her hair was silver now, long and flowing, and it suited her better than when she had dyed it black.

She raised her glass at him. "You came back in time for the fun."

He set the backpack down on the low wall separating the condos from the beach two feet below. The wind was picking up, waves pushing high onto the sand. Once, he'd paced out the distance between his condo and the water—sixty to seventy yards at low tide, but at high tide, sometimes less than ten.

"I hope a little fun is all we get. You're boarding up, right?"

"Oh, Peter, you know me better than that." Maggie threw her head back and laughed. "I've got some guys coming in the morning, if they don't flake out on me."

"Let me know if that happens," he said, turning the key in the lock.

She laughed again. "You gonna come to my rescue, Petey? With that hinky back of yours?"

He wagged a finger in her direction. "Be nice, Maggie. Don't forget who hauled you out of the water that time you went paddleboarding."

Maggie faked a pout. "How long you going to hold that against me? I had a leg cramp."

"Board sports and chardonnay don't mix, is more like it," he scoffed.

Maggie sniffed. "Now you're just spreading rumors."

Peter tapped his house key against his lips. "Your secrets are safe with me, Maggie. You know that." For good measure, he winked. "Did I miss anything while I was gone?"

She snorted loudly. "Well, you missed all the commotion at the Boat & Tackle. One of Marty's renters got stung by something while he was out fishing, and they took him away in an ambulance. Sue said he was in bad shape."

"You're kidding! Stung by what?"

Maggie shrugged. "They didn't know. Maybe it was a stingray?"

"We've got bat rays, but they're mostly found in quiet places like Elkhorn Slough in Moss Landing, not out in the open water."

There was always a first time, but he doubted it.

Inside the small entryway, he kicked off his shoes, then dropped the backpack on the coffee table in the tiny living room.

The view never got old—an expanse of water stretching all the way to the opposite side of the bay. If the windows opened, which they did not, he could have swung himself over the wall and onto the sand, and in seconds, he'd be standing under the old wooden pier.

The tide was still low, but the sky was an ominous gray.

They must have closed the beach. There wasn't a single person on the sand, and no boats moored near the pier either. The waves were empty too, but that wasn't unusual. Surfers preferred Fickle Point just around the bluffs.

He headed downstairs to take inventory.

The basements in the San Refugio Ocean Condos originally contained a bedroom and bathroom, but after repeated flooding, Peter had given up. His place was closest to the water and the first to flood during big storm surges, so he had poured cement on the floors and halfway up the walls and installed a sump pump in the corner. That way, when the ocean barged in, he didn't much care. No wood floors to ruin. No nice furniture or electronics to fuss over. Everything down there, like his surfboards and kayaks, could float.

Carla hated the basement. Said it made her crazy, such a nice space wasted. But Peter saw no point in paying good money for a storage unit when the basement had two rooms he didn't use.

With its unpainted cement walls, the downstairs had a bunker-like feel to it. If it weren't for the natural light from the high windows, it would have been downright gloomy. After the last big flood had turned the basement into a briny indoor pool, he'd been tempted to plaster over the windows, but the homeowners association had refused his request, so that was that.

Peter stepped over the kettlebells on the last step and crossed the room to a stack of plywood sheets leaning against a wall, each cut to fit one of his windows. They were all there, but he needed more. This time, he wanted to board up the inside too, even though it would mess up his trim. Double the protection.

That would require another trip to the hardware store, and he already needed to stop at city hall to pick up sandbags.

His back twinged in protest.

Peter was doing all he could to prepare, but it was a losing battle against Mother Nature, no matter how hard he tried to keep her out. Maybe it was time to give up. Sell the place to people with more money than sense. Get out before he ended up losing his biggest asset to a changing climate and the hungry sea.

Besides, if he stayed there, he'd never convince Carla to move in with him. Just getting her to spend the night was enough of a challenge. It was too close to the water, she had said, and it creeped her out. So, their relationship continued in limbo.

He went to the window and stared outside.

A chill swept across him, and his chest tightened. His throat felt funny too, like he couldn't swallow. *Jesus.* What the hell was happening to him? That's all he needed. A heart attack.

Behind the thick glass, the ocean was a low, steady murmur. Even with the looming storm, the water still drew him in. He'd never find another place like this. Before going upstairs, he took one last look, knowing the view just might be the death of him.

Chapter 3

overcast
winds gusting to 15 mph

Despite the gathering storm, locals still came to eat, drink, and gossip at Pancha's Restaurant. Carla preferred to hang out behind the bar, listening and soaking up the company from a safe distance. Unlike Peter, who enjoyed being in the middle of things, as he was now, sitting at a table talking about storm preparations and the tourist who got stung on the boat.

Peter was just about as different from her self-absorbed ex-husband as any man could get. He was a real people person, and everyone was drawn to him.

Unlike her. Carla had withdrawn when her son died.

After the accident, Peter started showing up for meals just before closing time. It was an obvious ploy if ever she saw one, but Carla was lonely and miserable, and Peter was a good listener. He had let her talk about Jacob as much as she wanted without once saying her son was in a better place.

The bottom of the Monterey Bay was *not* a better place.

With finances tight, she had moved into the second-floor apartment above the restaurant. The space had required some work to turn it into a proper home, but it was perfect: two tiny bedrooms, a small but cozy living room, a microscopic bathroom, a kitchen, a balcony, and an incredible view of the Monterey Bay.

The view was also a painful reminder of the son she'd lost.

"Are you sure you don't want to rent it out and move somewhere else in the village?" Peter asked when she'd announced her plan.

"Is that the healthiest choice?" her therapist had asked.

No, she didn't. And no, it wasn't.

But something compelled her to stay. A feeling she could admit to no one. Not to Peter. Not to her therapist.

The feeling Jacob wasn't dead.

Carla was wiping down the menus when the front door opened, letting in a gust of wind. It was Quint—a wiry man of medium height, thirtyish, with sharp features and brown hair.

"Please tell me I can have a burrito. I'm starving."

"You're always starving," she muttered, giving him a friendly shove toward the back table where the others sat.

"Yo," he called across the room. "That was pumpin' out there."

Carla stuck her head through the kitchen door. Gilbert and the other cook were there, doing prep. She wondered if it was a good idea to open for dinner, or the next day at all, for that matter.

"Can you do an extra large carnitas for Quint?"

Gilbert held up a massive tortilla. "We roll the fatties," he said, then laughed at his own joke.

Quint threw himself into a chair. "Can I please have a Modelo, Carla?" He brought his hands together in a pleading gesture.

She flapped a hand at him. It irked her that some people treated her as if she were a time bomb that could go off at any moment. As if being overly courteous would be enough to keep her from lashing out.

When she set the bottle on the table in front of Quint, Peter slipped an arm around her waist, and she felt herself stiffen. His head snapped up in surprise, hazel eyes widening. Carla still wasn't used to his public displays of affection. Her ex hadn't been the type to even hold her hand when other people were around.

Why did she always have to be so uptight? She gave Peter's hand a reassuring pat. A hint of a smile tugged at the corner of his mouth, and his shoulders relaxed.

For such a good-looking man, Peter was remarkably sensitive. Something she was still trying to get used to.

"Did you see the picture?"

All eyes stared up at her. Besides Peter and Quint, there was Ken Bigg, owner of Bigg's Bar next door.

Peter handed her the phone. Her nose wrinkled as she stared at the image.

Dear God. What the hell would do that to a person? The man's forearm had a hole surrounded by a glistening black ring, the skin turned an otherworldly shade of purple, slightly iridescent. There were smears of blood too.

Ken was practically floating with excitement. "Everyone is saying they've never seen anything like it." He shifted in his seat and turned to Quint, who'd just taken a bite of his burrito. "You were there. Did the guy say anything?"

Quint swallowed. "No. He was unresponsive by the time we got to him. They'll be doing toxicology tests, so that should tell us something, eventually. They moved him to ICU the last I heard."

"His girlfriend is a nurse at the hospital," Ken said helpfully, as if Quint and his girlfriend weren't regulars at Carla's restaurant.

She ignored him and turned to the firefighter. "So, it was venomous?"

"Oh, definitely. But it's a mystery."

Peter frowned. "A big mystery. There are lots of venomous fish. Stonefish, lionfish, pufferfish. But they mostly live in the tropics, and even if one happened to survive in this cold water, none of them would make that kind of wound."

Ken was practically bouncing in his chair. "It could be a new species."

Carla eyed the table and counted three empty beer bottles next to his plate.

He continued. "It could be those scientists near Moss Landing have been conducting secret experiments. You know, creating hybrids, and one of them escaped…"

Peter groaned. "And here we go."

"Oh, come on," Ken cried. "You don't think those scientists do stuff like that? Of course, they do. Haven't you ever heard of a liger? A zorse? What about the grolar bear? Have you ever seen pictures of the geep?"

"What the heck is a geep?" Peter laughed.

Ken's cheeks colored, and his lips curled in a snarl. "It's a sheep and a goat all mixed up. Now listen, I'm serious. Have you seen the size of those buildings they've got down there at Moss Landing? They're huge. What do they need all that space for? I tell you, they're doing some kind of secret experiments, and now one of 'em got out and did that." He pointed at the phone. "And I'm going to prove it!"

The smile vanished from Peter's face. "What do you mean 'prove it'? How?"

Ken lowered his gaze and didn't answer.

Carla felt Peter's hand spasm against her waist.

"Kenneth," Peter began sternly. "Do not, and I repeat, do *not* take your boat onto the water in this weather, looking for something that doesn't exist. The harbor master is not going to be happy if he has to send people out, risking their lives, to look for your sorry ass."

Ken lifted his hands into the air. Even his jowls managed to look smug. "That's not necessary. You'll see."

Peter and Carla exchanged uneasy glances.

"We'll see what?" Carla swept up the empty bottles, resisting the urge to crack one against the man's bald head. Ken always had that effect on her.

"All in due time," he said, tapping a finger against his chin.

"Like the time you said you saw a Lizard Man on the pier?" Peter snorted.

Quint laughed. "My favorite was the nose ring guy in the hoodie who was supposed to be a member of the Illuminati."

"Don't forget King Charles is a vampire," Carla added.

Ken's face flushed. He pushed back in his chair and got to his feet, balling his hands into fists. "I'm telling you, something is going on, and those meteorologists are in on it. That storm isn't as bad as they say it is because it's all a distraction from"—he sputtered—"the truth!" He slammed his hands down on the table, rattling the silverware and the remaining bottles.

Carla flashed a warning look at Peter not to goad him.

"Hey, Ken, you know this is just friendly banter. We're all neighbors here, having a little fun." Peter rose and put his hand on Ken's shoulder. "But you have to admit, a conspiracy of scientists is a little hard to swallow. I know some of those guys, and trust me, they're not that organized."

Ken narrowed his eyes. "You guys just accept whatever the media tells you, no questions asked, but what if there's something more? How would you know if you're not willing to listen to other ideas? Those scientists at Moss Landing could have the weather people in their pockets. They might all be in on it together. 'Cause every time one of those experiments gets out, here comes a storm!"

Carla stared at Ken. The man was losing it.

"Ken, please. Are you saying those people have the power to do…what? Create floods? That we're all imagining them? Because I had to fill out a lot of paperwork after the last one."

Ken shrugged. "Maybe. I don't know. It's complicated, and I'm just beginning to get a handle on it. But I will."

And with that, he swept out of the restaurant, chin in the air.

"Time for an interven…" Quint began. His voice drifted off, distracted by his phone chiming and vibrating on the table. He snatched it up and stared at the screen.

He scratched his jaw, frowning, then tapped out a response. Seconds later, his mouth fell open.

Carla gave his shoulder a little squeeze. "Everything all right?"

Quint shook his head. "Not really. The guy from the boat died. He turned purple all over and then had a heart attack."

Chapter 4

rain
wind gusting to 20 mph

After everyone had left, Peter was fidgety. His home was a constant source of stress, and Carla often wondered why he didn't sell it and buy a cottage high on the bluff, where he could see the ocean without being threatened by it. Of course, she could ask herself the same question and come up with the same answer.

Something compelled her to stay.

Peter wanted her to sleep at his place, but she declined, and he hadn't pressed the issue.

She could handle being so close to the water when the sun was out and the ocean behaved itself, but when a storm moved in and the waves began to crash against the shoreline, Carla felt a restless dread set in. It seemed like the sea was plotting to break through the windows and drown them all.

Of course, she'd invited Peter to stay with her, but her bed was too soft for his bad back, and she needed to get up early to meet her cousins' arrival to board up the windows. She'd told Peter they'd help him too.

She washed her face and changed into the shorts and tank she wore when Peter wasn't around. Both pieces were worn thin—the way she liked them. Carla climbed into bed, pulled up the comforter, and a moment later, kicked it off. Perimenopause was messing with her inner temperature gauge.

The wall between her place and the space next door was thin, and Carla could hear the muffled sounds of a video game, with its beeps, boops, chimes, and the occasional explosion. It wasn't too loud—at least, not loud enough for her to complain—but it reminded her of Jacob. He'd been obsessed with shooter games, which might have worried her if he hadn't been such a gentle soul.

If she'd known Ken was going to start renting out the crappy space above his bar he called a studio apartment, she would have renovated differently, switching the living room and bedroom so her head wasn't against a shared wall.

Her neighbor, Lucas Diaz, was nice. Very polite. His dad was a mechanic on a farm in Salinas, while his mother worked odd jobs. He was the first in his family to go to college. Or even graduate from high school, for that matter.

Ken Bigg was a little nutty, but he had a big heart. When he heard Lucas was commuting forty miles from Salinas to U.C. Santa Cruz every day because he couldn't afford student housing, Bigg had offered him the studio for two hundred bucks a month. An unbelievable deal, even for that dump.

Peter kept at her to hire Lucas because he needed the money and she needed the help. But the truth was, Carla couldn't bear to have him around. He reminded her too much of Jacob.

She tried reading for a while, but even her favorite British mystery author failed to hold her attention, so she set the book on her nightstand, turned off the lamp, and stared up at the ceiling. Carla really needed to sleep. Good sleep, not tossing and turning in a sweaty heap. Her heart was pounding like it was trying to break loose from her chest, which didn't help either. It was either the damn perimenopause or the glass of wine she had drunk while she and Peter watched the storm roll in.

Carla had just drifted off to sleep when she was startled back awake.

What the hell was that?

A distant, rhythmic slapping and thumping. It was coming from the east, too far away to be Lucas. Maybe some tourists blasting music in the vacation rental on the other side of Lucas's apartment.

She tried to ignore the noise, focus on her breathing and fall asleep, but the sound continued to grow louder. Carla sat up and listened intently. It was coming from outside, but it wasn't music, and it wasn't Lucas's video game.

Carla wondered if he knew what was causing the noise. It must be driving him crazy too. Together, maybe they could figure out how to stop it.

She swung her bare legs to the floor, fetched a rain jacket from the closet, and slipped it on. From under the bed, she grabbed the flashlight she kept in case of a power outage. They had plenty of those in San Refugio.

Carla shoved her feet into her sneakers and gasped when she stepped outside, feeling the force of the storm blasting against her face. The crashing waves were loud, but not loud enough to drown out the steady slap-thump. It was coming from somewhere down below, behind Ken Bigg's bar. He had a deck, too, and a gated-off space where he stashed extra plastic patio chairs and empty kegs.

The noise stopped for a few seconds, then resumed. It was like a heavy, meaty smack against a hard surface. Carla had heard something similar before, in the kitchen, when Gilbert threw a slab of flank steak down on the cutting board just before he tenderized it with a cleaver. She couldn't imagine what could make that kind of noise outside.

But if she was going to get any sleep, Carla needed to find out what was causing it and get it to stop.

She climbed over the balcony partition, muttering to herself. By the time she was standing in front of Lucas's sliding glass door, Carla was soaking wet. She knocked, feeling foolish for standing out there. When he didn't answer, she knocked louder.

"Hey, Lucas," she shouted. "It's me, Carla, from next door."

Moments later, the curtain slid aside, and Lucas peered out, hair tousled. His eyes widened when he saw her, and he slid open the door.

"Is everything okay?"

He didn't invite her in, but she wasn't about to continue standing there in the pouring rain, so she pushed past him, dripping onto the old floor tiles, and glanced around. The room had little furniture. Just an old lumpy couch, a white plastic card table with textbooks strewn across the surface, a cheap chair, and a coffee table. That was it. The small kitchen was spotless. Not a single cereal box or dirty dish in sight.

Lucas wore plaid pajama bottoms and a faded T-shirt with the university mascot, a smiling yellow banana slug.

The door was still open, wind blowing the rain in. She gestured outside.

"Do you hear that?"

He frowned, head cocked to the side. "Now I do. What is it?"

Carla bit her lip. "I was hoping you could tell me. Did Ken say anything about his storage area before he left?"

Lucas thought for a moment.

Now that Carla got a good look at him, the resemblance she'd imagined between her son and this young man

22

weakened. Jacob had had a Roman nose, like hers, and full lips. Lucas had smooth brown skin and delicate features. He was taller too.

"He didn't say anything to me," he said, reaching past her to slide the door closed. "Not really."

"What do you mean 'not really'?"

Lucas shrugged. "He told me to stay off the deck. He said it wasn't safe. Like, there might be a rogue wave or something."

Carla bit her lip. The chance of a rogue wave—even a giant one—making it that far up the beach was minuscule. But maybe that was Ken's way of making sure the young man didn't go snooping around. She opened the sliding door again.

Slap. Slap. Slap.

Lucas's eyes widened. "I have no idea what that is."

That did it. She dug her phone out of her pocket and punched in Ken's number. He answered on the fourth ring, sounding groggy.

"Wha?"

"It's Carla," she snapped.

"I know that." He paused. "Please don't tell me something happened to my place."

"Your place is fine," she reassured him. They had one thing in common: they both stood to lose a lot if something happened to their businesses. "But, Ken, there's a weird noise coming from downstairs, out back of the bar. You have any idea what it is?"

A long silence followed.

"Kenneth?" she said. Carla was cold and wet and wanted to go home, dry off, and get in bed.

He cleared his throat. "Well, a piece of driftwood got under the deck, and with all the rain and now the wind, it must be moving around down there, banging around into the pilings, and making a racket. I'm sorry about that, Carla. I should have seen to it before I left. Meant to. But I forgot."

Too busy obsessing over mad scientists and imaginary hybrid species, followed by one too many beers.

She sighed. "For God's sake, Ken, don't try and do it yourself. See if one of the guys from public works can get it out."

They hung up, and she explained what Ken had said. Lucas listened intently and then frowned, a deep crease forming between his eyebrows.

"Wait. So, this building isn't, like, on the ground?"

"No. None of the buildings on this part of Ocean View are. They're all on pilings, just like the pier. We're elevated above the sand and the creek, and when the creek rises or there's a really high tide, the water washes underneath. That's why there are staircases from all the decks down to the beach. You've never noticed?"

Lucas grinned sheepishly. "Nope. Not even once. But now I know."

Carla sighed. "Well, we'll deal with this tomorrow. Have a good night, Lucas."

She turned and left, climbing back over the railing, the rain pouring down.

Chapter 5

light rain
tide 2.3 ft

Peter eyed the water level under the pier while he waited for his coffee to brew. The rain had let up, turning into a steady drizzle. It was 7:00 a.m., and the tide was coming in.

The charts predicted king tides—extreme lows and extreme highs—for the next few days. King tides happened a few times each year and didn't usually cause any trouble, but watching the waves climb slowly up the beach made Peter nervous.

Where the pier ended, the service road began, and the San Refugio Ocean Condominiums ran right alongside it. On the rare occasion when waves inundated the pier, the water was funneled straight toward the road and the condo complex, with his unit front and center.

Peter lived in a sun-soaked bullseye.

But that hadn't happened since the mid '80s. He hadn't been there at the time, but he saw photos. The wedge-shaped front of Unit #1 had resembled the prow of a ship slashing through the surf. Except the condo was sitting still, and the surf was battering the stucco building.

Peter rubbed his lower back and sipped his coffee, staring at the gloomy, dark clouds over the bay. The twinge in his muscles was still there but barely.

When he got out of the shower, he saw he'd missed a call from Carla. He was about to return it when he saw her text.

Breakfast?

His stomach grumbled. *Hell yeah,* he replied.

At the entryway, Peter grabbed a rain jacket and left. Maggie was sitting in her easy chair by the living room window and waved as he went by. In return, he saluted and continued walking toward the historic San Refugio Bridge, which spanned Cortina Creek. He stopped at the ornate deco concrete railing and peered down at the rush of muddy water below.

A handful of locals and their dogs were there too, shaking their heads.

The torrent of brown water carried logs, branches, leaves, and other debris down from the hills. If the levels rose much more, all that stuff would jam up under the bridge, and the creek would overflow, inundating the village. The heavy rainfall had saturated the hillsides above San Refugio, and there had even been a couple of landslides.

An enormous log—a tree, really—floated under the bridge and out to the sea.

It was too early for San Refugio Charters to be open for business, but the lights were on. As he crossed the bridge, Peter could see Amalia pacing in front of the back windows overlooking the rushing creek. The tall blond had one hand on her hip and her phone pressed to her ear.

An empty shop with a For Lease sign in the window separated Amalia's business from Harmon's Fish Restaurant. Yuki Ito-Harmon stood outside smoking a cigarette under the blue and white awning.

"I thought you quit," Peter said.

Yuki took a long drag before answering. "We're booked solid for lunch, and I couldn't get to yoga this morning, so I'm doing this instead." She sighed. "I guess I should be grateful for the business, considering we'll have to close the rest of the weekend. You going to Carla's?" Yuki's long black hair sparkled with silver strands. Even in her cuffed jeans and clogs, she looked elegant.

Peter nodded.

Yuki flicked her cigarette butt onto the sidewalk and stubbed it out with her toe. "I did a stupid thing."

For a moment, Peter was distracted by the sound of rushing water coming from the storm drain. He returned his gaze to Yuki. "Something stupid? That doesn't sound like you."

Yuki shoved her hands into the pockets of her gray cardigan. "Matt thinks I was meddling." Yuki ran the restaurant with her husband.

Peter stiffened. "Is this anything to do with Carla and Amalia?"

Yuki squeezed her eyes shut. "I invited them over for drinks. It was supposed to be a lady's night with some other women. Amalia got here first, and then Carla walked in. Amalia said hello, but Carla wasn't having it. She turned around and walked right back out."

Peter groaned. Carla hadn't mentioned it, but that didn't surprise him. She held her grudge against Amalia long after the Coast Guard had cleared her of any negligence. Amalia, who had her captain's license, was responsible for the maintenance of her fleet, and Carla blamed her for the accident that had killed her son.

"When was this lady's night?" Peter asked.

"A couple days ago." Yuki dipped her head.

"You haven't talked to her since?" Carla and Yuki were best friends.

"No," Yuki admitted, eyes clouding. "But we've both been really busy." She paused. "She's been acting funny since Lucas moved in. I think he reminds her of Jacob."

"Yeah, probably so," Peter said glumly. When it came to Carla's grief, he felt helpless.

Yuki reached out and squeezed his arm. "I'll talk to her when things calm down."

Peter eyed the darkening skies. The rain had stopped, but more storm clouds were moving in, and it looked like they were in for another downpour.

"Okay, I hope things work out." He turned toward Carla's restaurant. "Take care with this weather."

Pancha's was open for breakfast. Normally, Carla only served breakfast on the weekends, but she was probably trying to do as much business as she could before the storm hit. The back tables were filled, mostly with locals. Two women he didn't recognize sat in a booth by the window with Carla taking their order.

She glanced in his direction and gestured toward the counter. Peter didn't know many women who looked as good as she did in jeans and a black crewneck sweater—her winter uniform. Carla's dark hair was pulled back in a low ponytail, a simple style that suited her face and high-bridged nose. His heart beat a little faster.

Jesus. She made him feel like a teenager.

He watched her bustling around the restaurant. She was like a shark—never stopped moving. When he first began visiting the restaurant as an excuse to see her, Peter had worried she was pretending to be busy to avoid him, but he soon realized she was doing the job of three people. Carla appeared willing to give him her attention after hours, but even then, she seemed to hold a part of herself back, just out of his reach. A sort of wariness, as if she wasn't sure she wanted to get more involved.

But getting more involved was exactly what he wanted.

A few minutes later, she was pouring him a coffee.

"You want to try a chorizo burrito this time?" she asked, a mischievous glint in her eyes.

He made a face. "Not after Gilbert said there's pig snout in it."

"Gilbert's just messing with you. We make it ourselves. It's snout-free." Carla crossed to the kitchen door and pushed it open with her shoulder. "Peter's here. Can you do his usual?"

When she returned, Peter leaned over the counter and kissed her on the lips. Her eyes widened in surprise.

"What did I do to deserve that?"

"I missed you last night," he admitted.

"Did you sleep okay? With your back?"

Peter shrugged. He hated talking about his aches and pains. It made him sound like an old man. "Yeah, fine." Taking in the dark circles under her eyes, he added, "How about you?"

Carla topped off her coffee and scowled. "Fuckin' Ken. Doesn't attend to shit like he should. There was this annoying banging sound that was driving me crazy, and I couldn't figure out what it was, and neither could Lucas. So, I called Ken, and he said it was a piece of wood smacking into the pilings."

Now it was Peter's turn to frown. "And you heard that all the way up in your place?"

"Yeah, I did. It was loud. Ken said he'd take care of it today. Gilbert saw him when he came in, but then he disappeared."

"Sounds like Ken."

Across the room, the two women began to laugh loudly. They were young. Around thirty. Too well dressed to be local. The kind of outfits tourists wore, thinking San Refugio was a highbrow beach community like Laguna, when it was more of a jeans and flannel kind of town.

Peter jerked his head in their direction. "Let me guess. Southern California?"

Carla smirked. "Yep. Said they work for a startup or something. They're staying at the vacation rental on the other side of Ken's bar."

"Are they checking out today?"

Carla shrugged. "They've got the place for the whole weekend. Waiting to see if we get evacuation orders, and if we don't, they're gonna stay."

Peter glanced over at the wall of windows. The sky outside was foreboding, a wash of deep gray and black. Still, it was beautiful. Like a moody oil painting. Peter didn't blame the tourists. He wouldn't want to leave either. And he'd been inside their rental. It was nice, with an updated kitchen and an electric fireplace.

He was pushing away his plate when he saw Yuki's husband, Matt, rushing past the back windows, shoulders hunched against the wind. Minutes later, Matt reappeared, pulling a cart loaded with boxes. Booze, probably. Matt had a deal with Ken to buy wine and liquor if they were running low, even had a key to Ken's place. For a moment, Peter considered offering to help but remembered his back and gave Matt a friendly wave instead. Matt shot him the finger, then grinned.

Peter had just finished his second cup of coffee when a bulldozer appeared on the beach and began shoring up the sand berm.

He wiped his fingers on a napkin, crossed the restaurant, and went outside to greet the public works director supervising the job. "Hey, Mark."

Mark had bright blue eyes in a long face creased from too much sun. "Hey, Peter. Looks like you might be in luck this time."

Peter felt a jolt of hope. "Oh yeah? What are you hearing?"

Mark nodded. "The forecasts are backing off the bomb cyclone. Looks like it's going to give us a miss. The real worry now is the creek. If the rain keeps up, it'll flood, but we've dealt with that before."

"So, no storm surge?"

"Not any more. Just a very high tide."

Peter exhaled with relief. "So, no evacuations? That's good news."

"It sure is. The last storm surge knocked us out. I was brand new back then, but I remember it like it was yesterday." Mark gestured to the dozer behind him. "Still, we're not taking any chances. We're going to continue reinforcing the dune."

It didn't work the last time, Peter thought but didn't say it.

Mark jabbed a finger toward the east. "The sheriff's office is going to send out an advisory to the residents along the creek. But anyone who's in an elevated building or has a second floor should be okay until the water recedes, so we're leaving it up to people to decide what they want to do." Mark paused. "That basement of yours could flood with you being so close to the creek."

"Probably will," Peter admitted. "But I'll take a flooded creek over a tidal surge any day."

He glanced into the restaurant. Carla was standing in front of the windows, head cocked to the side.

Peter gave her a thumbs-up, and she waved a menu in the air. Easy enough to guess what that meant. Carla knew Mark had the inside scoop on disaster preparedness.

"Carla wants to know if she'll be able to stay open for business."

Mark turned and waved at Carla. She waved back. He shrugged.

"Sure, as long as the water doesn't come up this far. As you know, sometimes it does; sometimes it doesn't. Even if the west end of the street floods, people can still get here by the back streets, or down Cortina Way."

Peter thanked him and was walking toward the restaurant when Mark called after him.

"Hey, Peter. I wouldn't stay at your place for the next couple of days if I were you. Just in case."

Chapter 6

overcast

Peter helped Carla bus dirty plates after the breakfast rush. He spotted Ken Bigg out on the sidewalk, talking to a young man with a crew cut and an expensive-looking camera hanging from a strap around his neck.

Ken kept glancing around nervously.

When the young man left, Peter sauntered outside, trying to appear nonchalant. "Hey, Bigg. What are you up to?"

Ken jumped. "Peter! Just chatting with a reporter about storm preps." He ran a hand over his fleshy face. "You know. The usual. Is global warming responsible for all the weird weather we've been having, and what are we doing to prepare for the storm."

Peter nodded, eying the brooding sky. "Kinda weird he didn't talk to Carla. Did he talk to Matt or Yuki?" When reporters came, they usually tried to get as many interviews as possible.

Ken shifted uneasily and shrugged. "I don't know."

"Where was he from? What news outlet?"

"He's a radio reporter, actually." Ken cleared his throat. "One of my favorite shows."

Peter raised his eyebrows. "You mean, the one with that idiot who talks about conspiracy theories?"

"They talk about other stuff," Ken snapped. "They're doing a story about how small businesses are preparing for extreme weather. The rate we're going, we'll all be underwater in ten years." Ken held up a hand to ward off a lecture. "It's good publicity for the bar. The off-season is rough, and I can use all the help I can get."

Peter shrugged. "I get it. Hey. Carla told me about that piece of wood below your place. You able to do something about it?"

Ken opened his mouth, then shut it again. His double chin quivered. "I'm on it, I'm on it. I just got here, for Christ's sakes. Carla's wound tighter than a two-dollar watch. You know what Carla needs? She needs a good—"

"Shut up, Ken," Peter interrupted. "What's wrong with you?"

Ken held up two chubby hands in a placating gesture. "Can't you take a joke? I was just joking."

"Well don't," Peter growled.

Ken did his best to look solemn, but Peter didn't like his expression. There was a smugness to it. He decided it was time to change the subject.

"Looks like the weather forecast is changing—"

It was Ken's turn to interrupt. "Heard that."

"Are you going to open tonight?"

Bigg chortled. "I haven't closed on a Friday night in five years since I took a week off to go to Mexico. Of course, I'm going to open."

With that, Ken shuffled into his place.

Peter stared after him. The conversation had been odd, even for Bigg.

At 2 o'clock, Peter and Carla stood on the back deck, debating whether to bring in the plastic patio furniture. If so, they'd have to wait until the dinner service was over and stash it all inside. Normally, Peter didn't hang out for long at the restaurant, but with all the questions about what the weather would bring, he wanted to be there. He wanted to prove he was serious about their relationship, and if that meant helping her out at work, so be it.

It had rained nonstop for the last several hours, and the sky was dark and menacing.

Lucas appeared on Bigg's deck, dark curls dancing in the wind. He smiled shyly. "I don't start my shift until four, if you need some help."

"We're fine," Carla said.

She could hardly bring herself to look at the kid, Peter noticed. He nudged her, but she ignored him and crossed her arms in front of her chest.

Lucas's shoulders slumped. "Okay. I'm around. I've been meaning to tell you that I used to work at my uncle's restaurant in Salinas. So, I can, you know, do stuff."

Carla's head swiveled toward him. "Wash dishes?"

"I can cook," he stammered, jamming his hands into his pockets. "I can wait tables too. Pretty much anything."

Carla could be intimidating. When Peter first met her, she had made him nervous too.

She gave a curt nod. "Good to know. I'll keep that in mind. In case anything opens up."

Peter gave her a sidelong look. She needed help. Badly. And here was the solution, literally living next door. Lucas could use the extra cash too. It would have been a perfect match if he hadn't reminded Carla of her late son.

Lucas's head bobbed up and down. "Yeah, that would be great. I'm around. School doesn't start for another two weeks."

Carla flashed him a chilly smile and gave him a thumbs-up as he turned to leave.

The patio door behind them slid open with a squeak. A young man wearing a royal blue all-weather jacket stepped out onto the deck.

"Are you Carla Ornelas? My assignment editor called you about an interview?"

Carla looked him up and down through narrow eyes. "Are you an intern?"

The young man grinned. "No, ma'am. I'm Eric Chen. I'm a reporter."

Peter couldn't help but stare. Eric Chen had black hair, high cheekbones, and an impossibly deep, resonant voice for someone so young.

Eric extended his hand to Carla. "Thanks for making time for me." He pointed to the beach. "How about if we do the interview out there, with the pier in the background?"

Carla accepted his handshake with a thin smile. "Sure."

Peter marveled at her nonchalance. In his many years as a park ranger, he'd always felt self-conscious in front of the camera. But Carla served on the city council, and the local media loved her. She was a natural.

As Eric screwed his camera into a tripod, Carla peppered him with questions. Eric had just started his job at the station after graduating from Cal State Chico. He grew up in Moss Landing, where his mother worked at a marine science lab. Peter was tempted to make a crack about secret experiments, but Eric had his eye on the viewfinder.

"All right, Carla. So here we go. Are you going to be closing and boarding up?"

Carla shook her head. "No. The last we heard, we're not under any storm advisories." She held up a hand. "Can we stop for a moment? I think there might be some confusion. The forecast has changed. I told your assignment editor that."

Eric winced. "Yeah, about that. I don't know if you watch our station or not, but our meteorologist, Bambi Mancuso, says the data is telling her something different. She says it's possible San Refugio is going to be hit with the bomb cyclone after all, and it may arrive at the same time as an extreme high tide."

Peter felt his jaw drop. He looked at Carla, expecting her to be as concerned as he was. Instead, she gave a dismissive sniff.

"Yeah, I've watched your meteorologist. No offense, but she tends to get a little too excited about severe weather. The city doesn't mess around. Can't afford to. I'm gonna trust their forecast over Bambi's."

Eric shrugged. "Well, that's my assignment. And they want me to do a live shot at five o'clock."

Carla's dark eyes snapped open. "I get it. You're supposed to do a story about how we're not going to be prepared because the city's got the forecast wrong. Is that it?"

"Well, if that's how things turn out…," Eric admitted, his tone sheepish.

"Then you shouldn't be talking to me. You need to talk to the mayor or the public works director."

"But—"

Carla stepped out of the frame. "I'll talk to you, but only after you get an official statement from the city."

Eric inhaled deeply before clearing his throat. "Yes, ma'am. Like Arnold says, 'I'll be back.'"

After he'd left, Peter watched Carla pace in front of the low wall separating the deck from the beach. Thunderous waves pounded the shoreline.

"Shit, Carla," he said. "What if they're right?"

Carla sucked air through her teeth. "Yeah, it's possible. Either way, it won't hurt to be prepared. We'll board up after dinner." She paused. "You need to stay here with me tonight. And we have to tell the others what he just said."

Peter rose slowly with a grimace. He really ought to take something for his back, but the only thing that worked made him sleepy. "I'll make the rounds."

Chapter 7

light rain
51°

Carla was rolling cutlery in napkins at the hostess station when the front door opened. It was Yuki, one clog over the threshold, peering in hesitantly as if seeking approval to enter.

"Hey." The simple word came out more stiffly than Carla intended.

Yuki's long straight hair fluttered in a gust of wind. "Have you seen Matt?"

"No. He hasn't been here. Why?" She impatiently waved Yuki inside.

Yuki pulled the door shut behind her, biting her lip. "I don't know where he is. And he's not answering his phone. It goes straight to voicemail."

"That doesn't sound like him," Carla said. "When did you last see him?"

Yuki thought for a moment. "Almost two hours ago. We were cleaning up after our lunch party, and Matt was restocking the bar. And then he was gone."

Carla crossed the dining room and stood at the bottom of the stairs leading up to her apartment.

"Hey, Peter," she called.

Peter had gone upstairs to sit with a heat pad on his back. He emerged a moment later, blinking, dirty blond hair tousled. It looked like he'd been napping.

"Have you seen Matt? Yuki doesn't know where he is." She turned so Yuki couldn't see her and mouthed, *She's worried.*

Peter scraped a hand through his hair. "I did see him, but not since this morning since he was headed back from Ken's place to pick up some booze."

Carla took a step back and turned to Yuki, who was absently biting a nail. "Have you checked with Bigg? Peter thinks he went there."

"He did, but he came back. I texted Ken, and he said he hasn't seen him."

Peter descended the stairs, grimacing as he gripped the rail. "Could he have gone home?"

The Harmons owned a cottage on Cortina Creek. It was close enough for them to walk to work, and Matt could easily have run home.

"I checked," Yuki said. "He's not there. I'm really starting to get worried."

Matt took medication for high blood pressure. He also had panic attacks. Yuki had been concerned the long hours and stress of running the restaurant had taken a toll on her husband. She often told Carla she worried he'd have a stroke.

Carla patted Yuki's arm. "He probably just went to pick up some sandbags or something, and his phone's out of a charge."

Yuki swallowed, blinking back tears. "The car's still in the driveway."

Carla gave Peter a pleading look, but he was already headed toward the rear deck. "Why don't I take a look around. Maybe he's talking to someone and just lost track of time. He's a chatty guy, right?"

Yuki nodded eagerly. Of the two of them, Matt was the social one.

Carla snatched Peter's jacket from a peg in the stairwell. It was drizzling again. Yuki followed Peter outside, with Carla right behind.

The wet, blustery weather, combined with the pounding of the surf, added to Carla's unease. Yuki's fear was palpable, like the mist from the drizzle dampening their faces. Matt was fine. Of course, he was fine. He hadn't been missing for that long, and Yuki tended to catastrophize her husband's health problems. Lots of people had high blood pressure.

There was probably a perfectly reasonable explanation, one they'd laugh over when he returned. Still, a knot of dread formed in Carla's stomach as she watched Peter walk toward Bigg's Bar. Yuki was trembling, so pale Carla was afraid she might faint. Carla tucked Yuki's cold hand under her elbow.

"He'll turn up," Carla said. "You'll see."

Peter stopped at the end of Bigg's deck and stared out at the water. Carla watched him scan the beach, from the back of the restaurant on his left, past the beach volleyball nets, over Cortina Creek, and to the pier and San Refugio Ocean Condos on his right.

And then he was running toward a mound at the shoreline.

It could have been a pile of seaweed or a seal. Yuki saw it too. She raced after Peter across the stretch of sand, black hair streaming behind her, Carla on her heels.

The shape was neither seaweed nor seal. It was a man lying face down in the wet sand, wearing tan cords and a navy-blue fleece jacket. His face was turned away from them, but when Carla saw the red hair, her heart sank. It was Matt.

Yuki pulled ahead and managed to turn Matt over.

His lips were blue, eyes vacant.

Yuki brushed the sand from his face, then yelled at Peter. "Do something! Help him!"

Peter lowered himself to his knees with some difficulty due to his back. Carla guessed he intended to start CPR.

"Please wake up! Matt, please!" Yuki cried as Peter pressed his hand on Matt's sternum.

Carla tried to pull Yuki away from the body to give Peter the space he needed to maneuver. That's when she spotted it. A hole on the right side of Matt's neck, ringed with a thick layer of black slime.

She grabbed Peter's arm and yanked him back so hard he fell sideways onto the sand. He glowered up at her, mouth opening to respond.

Carla pointed. His eyes followed and snapped wide when he registered the wound. Matt's skin had a strange purple cast to it, slightly iridescent near the gaping wound.

Yuki screamed. "No, no, no. What's that?"

Carla crouched next to Peter. "That's the same thing that happened to the tourist yesterday," she said in a low voice. "Stung by something. That's what Quint said. That's what this looks like, right?"

Peter brought his legs under him and slowly rose, one hand pressing into his back. "I think so." He patted his pockets. "I left my phone. Do you have yours?"

Carla nodded. Her ears were filled with Yuki's agonizing sobs, and her hands were shaking. She pulled the phone from her jeans and called 911.

Chapter 8

overcast

Carla watched the hubbub on the beach through the back window of the restaurant. Officers from police, sheriff's, and fire departments, even the coast guard had descended. They'd closed the beach. Yellow caution tape stretched across the entrances. Signs read: "Do not proceed beyond this point. Beach hazard."

At least the rain had stopped. Not for long, though. More clouds were moving in from across the bay.

Peter knew most of the officers and had gone over to join them. Carla could tell it bothered him not to be at the center of the action.

Yuki was upstairs in the tiny spare bedroom. She'd taken one of Matt's anti-anxiety meds, and the last Carla checked, she was curled up in a fetal position, face turned toward the wall.

There had been no need for Yuki to ride along in the ambulance that had taken her husband away. An officer informed them a multi-agency investigation would take place due to the nature of the wound.

The businesses along Ocean Drive were allowed to remain open, so Carla was readying for the dinner rush. Once the locals heard about Matt, they'd come to Pancha's, seeking the latest news.

Eric Chen, the reporter from the TV station, reappeared, asking Carla for an eyewitness interview about the discovery of Matt Harmon's body, but she refused. He was undeterred. Eric headed out to the beach, camera on his shoulder, and began interviewing an officer. When he was done, he disappeared into the news van.

At 4:45 p.m., Carla turned on the TV hanging over the bar. The dining room was nearly empty. Just a few locals sitting in a booth, sharing a plate of nachos and pondering what to order for dinner. The door opened, and Lucas appeared, book tucked under an arm. He nodded shyly and pointed at the counter.

"Can I get something to eat at the bar?"

"Of course," she said, wiping down the counter so she wouldn't have to look at him. "Aren't you working?" She slid a menu in front of him.

He shook his head. "Ken decided not to open after what happened. Plus, he said he's not feeling well."

Carla couldn't remember the last time Bigg's Bar didn't open on a Friday night. It seemed ominous somehow. She wondered if she should check on him. He lived alone in an apartment above Harmon's. Ken owned the building and leased the restaurant space to Yuki and Matt.

Oh God. Yuki couldn't handle the restaurant on her own. At least, not easily.

Carla took out her phone and sent Ken a text. The man was overweight, had diabetes, and drank too much.

She received a terse response seconds later: *I am fine. Thank you for asking.*

At least he wasn't dead. There was suddenly too much of that going around.

Lucas ordered carne asada nachos, and Carla's throat went so tight it was hard to breathe. He'd asked for Jacob's favorite dish.

At 5 o'clock, the newscast began, showing footage of San Refugio Beach and the caution tape that cordoned it off.

Carla shuddered, thinking about Matt lifeless on the sand, that horrible hole in his neck, Yuki weeping, the shock on Peter's face.

What the hell had happened?

Eric Chen had set up his camera on the stretch of deck between her restaurant and Bigg's place, his back to the action on the beach.

His deep voice was grave as he emphasized "the shocking and mysterious" nature of Matt Harmon's death, the second incident involving a venomous puncture wound. The other involved a forty-three-year-old man from San Jose, who had died with a similar injury after fishing near the San Refugio pier.

Carla's heart sank, realizing it was just a matter of time before more news crews arrived. It was a big story. One that would bring unwanted attention to the quiet town. Storm damage and floods brought out people eager to support local businesses during tough times. Shark attacks and things that killed people kept them away.

She was sipping club soda with lime when she heard Eric say, "While officials are tight-lipped about the incident, some locals wonder if a deadly sea creature lurks in the waters…"

"Whoa, whoa, whoa!" Lucas put down a corn chip smothered in cheese.

Carla coughed and glared at the TV screen. "Are you fucking kidding me?"

Lucas turned to her, eyes wide. "Who do you think is saying that?"

"Not anyone who owns a business in this village."

"Well, something did it, and it is freaky." Lucas pushed away his half-eaten plate of nachos.

Carla scooped the rest into a to-go container. "True, but it's irresponsible to start talking about sea monsters. And..."

Her voice drifted off. And what? What would make a big ugly hole in a man's neck like that? Something in the water. Something that injected venom. Toxic enough to kill. Carla felt a chill run down her spine.

The door opened, then opened again. The dinner rush had begun. It was an unusually big Friday night crowd—couples, families, some friends, all abuzz with the news about Matt Harmon.

Carla busied herself greeting customers, but it was hard doing double duty as hostess and server, and she struggled to keep up.

She was taking an order from a middle-aged couple who asked so many questions about the spiciness of the food, she wondered why they had bothered coming to a Mexican restaurant, when she saw Lucas emerge from the kitchen. He had an apron wrapped around his waist.

Carla was about to ask what the hell he thought he was doing, but the kitchen door opened again, and Gilbert appeared. His teenage grandson who helped on weekends stood directly behind him and waved.

"Hey, Carla," Gilbert shouted. "I asked Lucas if he could help us out tonight."

When she grimaced in surprise, Gilbert shot her a disapproving look and waved a dish towel in her direction.

Carla took a deep breath and tried to keep her composure as she finished taking the order. When she turned around, Lucas was seating the two women from the vacation rental, answering their questions about the incident on the beach. And doing a good job of reassuring them too. He might be tongue-tied around her, but he had an easy charm and a knack for conversation that belied his years.

Well, she needed the help. And he worked with a confidence that surprised her. Carla couldn't very well snatch away his apron and send him home. Might as well accept the help as gracefully as she could manage. Her son had hated helping at the restaurant, and when he did, he'd been awkward around customers. Lucas was anything but. The young man seemed to light up, moving between the tables and the kitchen.

After she'd poured a few beers from the tap at the bar, Carla shoved Lucas's leftovers into the fridge beneath the counter. No use all that food going to waste. There was enough there for another meal. She picked up his book from the counter before someone spilled beer all over it and noted the subject matter with some astonishment. Time management for college students—the kind of book she'd implored Jacob to read the summer before leaving for UC Santa Barbara, to no avail.

Eric Chen came in and ordered a burrito to go.

"Who told you that bullshit about a sea creature?" she asked, slapping the foil-wrapped bundle into his hand.

He shrugged. "Can't say. They didn't want to go on the record."

"Because saying that shit makes them sound insane."

"You'd be surprised," Eric replied.

"By what?"

"By who's doing the talking."

Carla gave him a long, hard stare. She reached into the fridge and retrieved a small plastic tub of salsa. Extra hot. "The tin foil hat should have been a tip-off."

Eric shook his head, frowning. "I know you're not going to believe this, but it's my reputation too. You don't know me, but I'm not going to put someone who's unreliable on the air just because they say something that might be good for ratings. My source is solid."

"Is that right?"

"That's right," he said pleasantly. "Excuse me, but I didn't get lunch, and I'm starving, and I have to set up for my next live shot."

By six o'clock, a TV news crew had arrived from San Jose, which meant the San Francisco stations couldn't be far behind. The crew cut through the alley between Pancha's and Bigg's Bar and headed to the beach. It was nearly dark out. Lampposts cast a warm yellow glow, illuminating the mist.

The officers had fanned out along the shoreline, flashlight beams sweeping across the sand and the incoming tide, looking for whatever had killed Matt.

A group of locals gathered around the bar to hear Eric Chen's report. He repeated his claim about a deadly creature but, this time, went further.

He said he'd spoken to a marine biologist who'd analyzed photos of the puncture wounds and said the injuries were similar to those made by stingrays. Except these were much, much larger.

Which meant, he said, whatever killed Matt was something nobody had ever seen before.

Chapter 9

light rain
wind gusting to 15 mph

Peter, cheeks reddened by the wind, hair standing up, walked in the back door of Pancha's, shaking his head. He collapsed onto a barstool, shoulders sagging.

Carla handed him a clean bar towel and watched as he dried his face. When he'd shrugged out of his jacket, she said, keeping her voice low, "You won't believe what Eric Chen just said on the air."

Peter rubbed the side of his face. "I heard. I was there when he asked the sheriff for a comment about a sea creature. A *sea creature*. Jesus. He wouldn't say who he talked to or how they got hold of a picture of the wounds."

"It's probably Sue. She took a picture of the guy who rented their boat."

Peter groaned. "That's right. I forgot. Who knows how many people she sent it to. And any of them could have shared it too."

"The picture is all over social media," Lucas said, joining Carla behind the bar.

Peter sighed loudly. "Of course, it is."

Lucas pulled his phone from an apron pocket, scrolled, then held it out for them to see.

Carla's eyes flicked over the screen and winced. So did Peter. It showed a close-up of ravaged skin. The wound was disgusting. Not a clean, neat little hole. Nearly the size of a golf ball. Beyond the viscous black ooze surrounding the wound, the flesh was an angry shade of red and puffy.

She turned away, swallowing.

Lucas continued staring at his phone. "Whoa. This one post says some biologists are coming out tomorrow to see if they can find it." He scrolled some more. "This story is all over the place. Everybody is talking about it."

Carla glanced over at Peter. This was a big event, the kind that used to get his adrenaline pumping. But now that he was retired, his face was etched with worry, a hint of uncertainty lurking at the corners of his hazel eyes.

She poured him two fingers of her best scotch, neat. He reached out and squeezed her hand. His fingers were still cold from being outside.

Outside. She'd lost track of the storm system after they'd found Matt Harmon on the beach. When she glanced over her shoulder at the TV, the anchor was introducing the station's meteorologist.

"Bambi Mancuso joins us live from San Refugio, where local officials are predicting the bomb cyclone will miss the village. Bambi?"

For once, the meteorologist appeared, not in an eye-popping dress, but in a blue jacket with her hair scraped back in a ponytail.

A single light illuminated the fine rain falling in front of the woman's face. Bambi seemed unfazed. "That's right. The sheriff's office currently has no plans to issue a warning to the residents and businesses along San Refugio Beach or Cortina Creek. These are the places that would be hit hard by a storm surge. Officials say their forecasts say the worst of the storm will pass to the south, so they aren't expecting the potentially disastrous combination of a storm surge and an extreme high tide. But I've been monitoring this storm with our new Storm Tracker 11…"

Lucas turned to Carla. "Aren't you going to board up?"

She pressed a finger between her eyes. Her cousins had never shown up. So now, there was no one to help install the boards at her place or Peter's. And Peter couldn't do it alone. Not with his back. What a mess. And it was getting late.

She explained the situation.

"I can do it," Lucas said eagerly. "As soon as we close. Gilbert's grandson can help me."

Peter pulled a wad of bills from a pocket and counted out forty bucks. "Can you help me out too? I'm around the corner at the condos."

Lucas nodded, went into the kitchen, and emerged a few minutes later. He grinned and gave a thumbs-up. "We can do it, no problem."

He ignored the money on the counter, Carla noticed. She added forty dollars to the pile and shoved it at him. "We don't make people work for free around here," she said sternly.

"Lew-kiss," a voice called from the row of booths.

Carla turned. The two women from the vacation rental were holding up empty wine glasses and making pouty faces.

"How much have they had to drink?" she said.

Lucas grimaced. "Whoa. Like, a lot."

"At least they don't have far to walk," Peter said.

A timid voice called out from the stairwell leading to the upstairs apartment. "Carla?"

It was Yuki, hair mussed, feet bare.

As Carla rushed toward her, Yuki said, "I'm sorry to bother you in the middle of dinner, but there's a loud banging coming from next door." The grief was still fresh on Yuki's face, her voice flat and distant.

51

Carla tipped her head back and groaned. "It's a piece of wood stuck under Ken's deck. He said he'd take care of it, and of course, he hasn't."

"It doesn't sound like that to me. It's too…rhythmic." Yuki paused. "Are you sure it's okay if I stay the night?"

Carla squeezed her friend's arm. "Of course. And besides, with the creek rising, you shouldn't be there anyway."

The Harmon's single-story cottage sat just a few feet above Cortina Creek and flooded when the water got too high. Yuki gave a vague nod and padded back upstairs, arms hanging limply at her sides.

The voices in the restaurant suddenly seemed louder and more intense. Words from the TV mixed with conversations and ranchera music coming from the kitchen. *"Storm surge…catastrophic flooding…jet stream…warmer ocean waters…"*

Carla tuned it all out. Something unknown had come from the water and killed Matt. What other explanation could there be?

Chapter 10

wind gusting to 35
tide 6.8 ft

Carla tapped out another text to Peter. When he didn't reply, she tried calling him again. Lucas had returned from boarding up the windows at Peter's place more than an hour ago. The last she'd heard from Peter, he'd texted to say he'd come over after he'd showered. Since then, not a word.

After two deaths, she couldn't help but worry. Peter had promised to stay away from the beach, but his condo was just steps from the sand, and if there was something out there capable of poking holes in people and killing them…

Had she lost her mind? What was she thinking? That there was some kind of new species out there, attacking people? If so, that made her as crazy as Ken Bigg, with his nutty theories about the labs at Moss Landing. Her apartment was warm, but she suddenly felt a chill.

Why wasn't Peter answering? Maybe his back gave out in the shower, and he was flat on the floor, unable to get to his phone and call for help.

Carla went into the kitchen, stepped outside onto the balcony, and squinted at the San Refugio Ocean Condos. It didn't look like anyone was outside. And why would they be, in this weather?

She checked her phone again. Still nothing. It wasn't like him to ignore her texts. After a career in public service, he always had his phone handy. Old habits die hard, he had said. And he always replied to her promptly. That was Peter.

Which only deepened her fear something bad had happened. Well, she wasn't going to wait around to find out. He lived a short walk away. She'd go over there and check on him.

"Come on, Peter," she muttered, calling again.

Carla couldn't sit still. She needed to see if he was all right. If he didn't answer the door, she'd use her key to let herself in.

She was reaching for her rain jacket when her phone screeched and shook in her hand. Startled, she nearly dropped it. The horrible noise seemed to go on forever. An emergency alert.

Heart pounding, she read the text.

STORM SURGE WARNING: Possible property damage and life-threatening inundation. Rising sea levels expected. Evacuate low-lying coastal areas immediately. Follow local officials' instructions and watch your local news for updates.

Yuki appeared in the doorway, disheveled and pale, clutching her phone to her chest. "Do we need to leave?"

Carla glanced toward the ocean and the dark and rising tide. "I don't think so. The weather forecast said the worst would miss us. Besides, we're on the second floor. The warning is probably more for people along the creek. If the water rises, the restaurant might flood a little, but we'll be too high for it to reach us. We might be stuck for a day or two, but we should be fine." She shrugged. "We could try to find a motel somewhere if it would make you feel better. It's up to you."

She hoped Yuki would say no. Spending money on a motel felt like an overreaction. The restaurant had flooded during the last big storm in the '90s, but the water that made it inside had quickly receded.

"What does Peter say?" Yuki's voice was low and scratchy.

Carla hesitated. She didn't want to alarm Yuki, but she didn't want to lie either. "We'll find out soon."

Yuki frowned. "He's not back yet?"

"Not yet."

Before Carla could say anything else, a knock on the living room's sliding glass door startled her. It was Eric Chen, the reporter, with Lucas at his side.

She opened the door, and cold rain splashed against her face. "What are you still doing here?" She pulled them inside and slid the door shut.

Eric offered a thin smile. "The storm surge. We knew it was coming, so I stayed."

"You're still sticking with Bambi's forecast? That alert didn't say the storm had changed direction."

Eric smiled. "Well, we'll find out soon."

Carla shifted her gaze to Lucas, who was looking uneasy. "And you're giving him a front-row seat to whatever happens?"

Lucas shrugged. "I'm tagging along. I thought it would be interesting. Is that...a problem?"

Carla hesitated, biting her lip. Eric Chen was only doing his job, and Lucas had every right to invite whoever he wanted, as long as they didn't bother her. But there they were, in her apartment.

She leaned in and spoke in a low voice. "Okay. So, what can I do for you? And don't even think about asking my friend for an interview. She just lost her husband."

Eric shook his head. "No, no, of course not. We were just wondering if we could grab some coffee."

"I ran out at my place," Lucas added with a sheepish shrug.

"You could buy some at the store, you know," she said to Eric. "You're going to have to move your news van anyway. If Bambi is right, it'll float away."

"I already moved it. Up to San Refugio Heights. I was hoping not to go back out again. The balcony is the ideal place to set up. I might miss some good shots if I leave."

Carla could hear Yuki rummaging around in the kitchen. She appeared a few moments later, holding a near-empty cannister of coffee.

"You're almost out," Yuki said.

As much as Carla was relieved to see Yuki upright and functioning, Lucas and Eric still annoyed her. Both were young enough to be her sons. Both were watching her expectantly, as though she could solve any problem they had. First it was coffee. Next, they'd be asking her to make them a snack.

"I'll go grab some coffee downstairs." Even to her own ears, she sounded put out.

"I can do it," Lucas said eagerly. "I know where it is."

"You can both come with me," she replied stiffly. Carla wasn't about to leave Eric alone with Yuki.

While she was down there, she decided to grab some extra food, just in case. If things took a bad turn, like she feared, she'd have Peter and Yuki to feed. Lucas probably didn't have much food in his place, so as much as the idea irritated her, she'd bring up enough for him too.

If the restaurant flooded, she'd have to wade all the way to the kitchen and hope the staples stayed dry. Which reminded her. She'd forgotten to check if Gilbert had moved the perishables from the bottom to the top shelves. If not, she'd ask Lucas and Eric to do it.

If they were going to treat her like their mom, she was going to give them chores.

They were downstairs less than two minutes when the lights went off, plunging them into darkness. Carla froze.

"There goes the power," Eric said.

Without the hum of refrigerators and ceiling fans, the sounds of the storm took over her senses.

Outside, the rain had increased in intensity, the drops hitting the glass as if trying to break through. The wind pushed against the windows, found its way around doors, and howled through the eaves.

Carla's pulse pounded, and she fought to maintain her composure. They'd lost power. That was nothing unusual in San Refugio. She had a backup generator and could connect the refrigerators if the electricity remained out for too long.

When she turned around, Lucas and Eric had their phones in the air with flashlights on, faces glowing white as they studied their screens. She glanced down at her own phone and instantly saw the trouble. No service. Which meant the cell tower wasn't working either.

She sniffed, heart sinking.

The odor was so faint, she hoped she was imagining it. "Do you smell anything? Is that gas?"

Lucas and Eric's heads lifted and turned, noses twitching.

"I don't smell anything," Eric said.

Lucas shrugged. "I don't know. Maybe."

That's not what she wanted to hear.

Carla pulled the kitchen door shut behind them, crossed the dining room to the back door, pushed it open, and peered outside. Even in the darkness, she could see angry, wind-whipped whitecaps across the wide expanse of bay. Closer to shore, mist blew off the tops of breaking waves.

They surged toward her, climbing higher and higher up the beach.

Chapter 11

heavy rain
storm surge 7.9 ft

Lucas helped Carla carry bags of food and supplies upstairs to her apartment. Yuki started putting things on shelves. Carla didn't object. After her son died, she hadn't been able to get out of bed, but everyone was different. The simple chore seemed to be doing Yuki some good. She moved quickly and with purpose.

Eric Chen had stepped outside, pointing his video camera at the ocean. The waves were breaking halfway up the beach.

Carla put on her jacket and joined him on the deck, positioning herself just under the overhang. The wind was fierce. The ocean roared.

A voice from above called her name, so she looked up. Ken Bigg was leaning over the railing of his apartment balcony above Harmon's restaurant.

"You guys shouldn't be outside," he shouted over the commotion of the storm.

She shot him a thumbs-up. "We're fine for a while yet."

"I'm serious, Carla. Go inside. It's not safe out here."

Carla pointed her flashlight at Ken. The beam caught his wide, frightened eyes. His face was red and sweaty. The man was practically hyperventilating.

Even with the storm bearing down on them, she couldn't resist a dig. "I thought you said the storm was invented by the marine scientists."

Ken waved a hand over his head. "No, no, no. Carla, for once, would you listen to me? Please. Go back inside. The both of you. You know what happened to Matt and that other guy? Whatever did it could be out there, and it's dark, for Christ's sake."

Ken was pleading now.

Eric shifted position and pointed the camera at Ken. Even with the waves advancing on the beach, Ken was the real show.

What had gotten into the man? His rising panic made Carla uneasy. Ken was clinging to the balcony railing, his heavy body swaying back and forth, his mouth open wide as if preparing to scream.

"Are you okay, Ken?" Maybe his blood sugar levels were off, causing erratic behavior. "Have you taken your insulin?"

He waved a hand at her. "I'm fine. Go. Back. Inside. Trust me when I say it's not safe."

Eric tensed beside her, glancing around nervously. "Maybe we should listen to him."

She wasn't inclined to argue. "It's miserable out here anyway."

Ken wasn't done yet. "Where's Peter? I need to talk to him."

Carla shivered. Her face was wet and cold from the rain. "He's not here yet. He's probably on the way."

"He better hurry if he doesn't want to get cut off." And with that, he went inside.

Carla wondered who else was weathering the storm along Ocean View Drive. She descended the steps to the sand. Sea water lapped over her feet and sloshed under the deck's floorboards. She turned and stared up at the row of buildings.

The vacation rental next to Lucas's place had a small portable generator. A single lamp burned by the window. The two women who had been in the restaurant earlier stood in the window and waved when they spotted her. She waved back. The taller of the two raised a wine bottle. Not a great time to drink, but what else were they going to do up there?

Ken's place was illuminated by a warm amber glow. Battery-operated lanterns, probably. She had some in the closet and made a mental note to retrieve them.

On the other side of Ken's building, more light spilled from the tall windows of Amalia's place. Which meant she'd powered up her portable generator. She lived alone in the apartment above her business now that her son and daughter were away at college.

Eric Chen had started filming her, but Carla ignored him.

"Why don't you come in?" Eric called from the deck, lowering the camera. It had a plastic cover to protect it from the rain. The gusts whipped the jacket's hood from his head.

Was she imagining things, or did he sound almost as nervous as Ken? Being close to a major storm was unnerving. She thought of Peter and felt her throat tighten. Where the hell was he?

Her eyes itched and watered. She took a deep breath. Now was not the time to fall apart. The waves were getting bigger and closer, and she felt the salty mist of the sea on her face.

She was about to go in when she heard it. A racket coming from the back of Bigg's Bar, muffled by the roar of the surf. It sounded like things were getting knocked over—tables, chairs, the clang of metal kegs banging together. Maybe an animal had gotten into the enclosure where Ken stashed extra patio furniture. She couldn't imagine what could be causing all that noise. Her skin prickled.

The noise stopped.

Carla strained to listen, but all she could hear was her pulse pounding in her ears, the waves crashing against the shore, and the howling of the wind.

Whatever it was, this was not the time to investigate. She locked the door, swinging her flashlight around the restaurant in one final check before heading upstairs. Yuki must have found the lanterns because there was light coming from the kitchen.

When she entered, Yuki was pouring Eric and Lucas coffee as they sat at the small table. At least the gas was still on.

Yuki held up the carafe. "It's still hot. Want some?"

What Carla really wanted was a giant glass of red wine. Something to steady her nerves. But she needed her wits about her, so she nodded. Yuki's hands trembled slightly as she handed Carla a steaming mug. Carla wondered how long Yuki would last before retreating into grief. It had been less than eight hours since the ambulance had taken her husband's body.

They drank their coffee in silence. Carla could feel Lucas watching her.

"I can go check on Peter if you want."

She bit her lip. It was a tempting offer, but in the darkness, it was hard to tell how far the tide had come in. If it was too high, Lucas could get swept away. The same was true for Peter if he tried to reach the restaurant.

Carla shook her head, then went to the patio door and opened it. The storm rushed to meet her, rain lashing her face. She gritted her teeth and squinted, staring out at the water.

Nothing but blackness. Pointing the flashlight downward, she saw the waves had reached the restaurant, lapping against the door and the bottom of the boarded windows. She could hear water rushing through the passageway between her place and Bigg's. The San Refugio Ocean Condos must already be inundated.

There was no way Peter could make it now.

Chapter 12

winds gusting to 53 mph

A thundering boom woke Peter with a start. It was so dark he didn't know where he was. He swept a hand across the bed.

Alone. Home.

And then he remembered.

After Lucas boarded up the windows, the pain in his lower back had gotten so bad, Peter'd taken a muscle relaxant. No, two. Which he never did. Then he'd stretched out on the bed to take a short nap.

Jesus. What time was it? What had made that sound? Whatever it was had shaken the walls. Then he heard the wind. And the surf booming and crashing, like it was right outside his window.

Peter reached for the light on the nightstand. Nothing. The power must have gone out. Not a good sign.

From the top drawer, he grabbed a flashlight and flicked it on. His phone had fallen on the floor. When he bent to pick it up, his back didn't protest, which meant the pills were still working. And explained why his head felt thick and fuzzy.

Peter squinted at the screen and groaned. Just past midnight. The display showed missed calls and texts, all from Carla, starting with *Hey? Where are you?* and ending with *PETER! WTF? I'm freaking out.*

Any other time, he would have welcomed this small proof Carla's feelings for him were more than just casual affection. But tonight, he hated to think he'd caused her unnecessary panic. The last time someone hadn't responded to her texts and calls, it had ended in the worst way possible: the discovery that her son had been killed in a freak accident.

Peter had plenty of charge left on his phone but no service. He could guess what had happened. During severe storms, high winds and saturated ground sent trees crashing down, and sometimes, those trees took out homes, power poles, and cell towers.

He needed to see what was happening outside, but every window was boarded up. As he felt his way down the hall, a surge of anxiety rippled through him, helping to clear the brain fog.

At the top of the stairs leading to the basement, he froze.

Water sloshed around below, and objects smacked into the walls. Taking a deep breath, Peter descended to the concrete landing and swept his flashlight across the room. The ocean was pouring in through the windows. The plywood had failed against the relentless onslaught of water. Seeing the flooded basement sent his pulse racing. His favorite surfboard, the color of bleached bones, glowed eerily as it bounced toward him. It slammed into the wall with a thud before shooting away.

Back upstairs, he pointed the flashlight at the three windows in the front room—still holding steady against the storm and sea. He'd told Lucas not to bother hammering boards on the inside, given the downgraded weather forecast, but now he regretted it.

Peter dreaded what awaited him outside, but he had to get to Carla.

In the entryway, he stopped to take stock. He'd fallen asleep in jeans and a T-shirt. Getting across the bridge to Ocean View Drive might be a challenge, and he'd be soaked by the time he got there. For a moment, he was tempted to put on his wetsuit, but he'd gained fifteen pounds since he'd last worn it, the weight mostly around his middle, and he doubted he could zip it up.

That was the price he paid for letting himself go. The extra weight wasn't doing his back any favors either.

Peter slipped on lightweight hiking boots, a hoodie for warmth, and a waterproof rain jacket, pulling up both hoods and securing them beneath his chin.

He cautiously opened the front door and made his way down the steps to the sidewalk. More than a foot of seawater was rushing down the path toward the beach. If that much water was receding, a very big wave must have come over the beach and onto the pathway just seconds before.

The wind howled around him, raindrops slapping his skin. He turned to his left and slowly walked up the sidewalk, feet and legs pushing against the rushing water. The roar of the storm assaulted his ears, and the strong salty brine in the air filled his nose. Peter kept his flashlight trained on the water rushing toward him.

Shit.

The path was completely flooded as far up as he could see, and there was debris in the water. The last thing he needed was a nail-covered two-by-four bashing into his shins.

Peter's mind raced. Getting past Cortina Creek, which had surely flooded, wouldn't be easy. And it could be dangerous. He aimed his flashlight across the creek toward the back deck of Carla's restaurant.

At that distance, the faint light revealed little. Peter squinted in the darkness. The king tide had come in as predicted, but the water was too high—just inches below the businesses along Ocean View Drive. The long width of beach was completely under water, and waves crashed over the rear decks, smashing into the walls of the buildings.

The extreme high tide was not the only force at play. A wind-driven storm surge was adding to the destructive power of the surf and waves, and the entire village of San Refugio was in its path.

The city had gone with the wrong forecast.

Chapter 13

heavy rain
winds gusting to 57 mph

Peter pointed his flashlight at Cortina Creek.

The downpour had drenched the hills above San Refugio. Rain landing on saturated ground flowed downhill in rivulets, then streams, then poured into the creek. The rushing water brought with it branches, trees knocked down by the wind, even patio furniture, all joining together in the swollen creek and hurtling past the condos toward the ocean.

Once there, huge waves, driven by the high tide and storm surge, picked up the debris and slammed it back on the shore with stunning force in a massive rush of water.

Carla knew this could happen, didn't she? She knew enough to stay upstairs, where she was safe. Didn't she?

They hadn't talked about it. Not specifically. He hadn't warned her. She'd just been a kid when the last big storm devastated the village of San Refugio, so would she recall how dangerous it could be? Peter knew. He had been a park ranger and state lifeguard, so he remembered what the powerful, angry ocean could do.

Peter felt like a fool for not having had a proper conversation with Carla before he'd left. He'd have to get over the bridge to Ocean View Drive as quickly as possible.

With waves lapping at the back of his knees, he shoved the flashlight into his jacket pocket and zipped it up, then lurched toward the bridge.

He hadn't made it a yard before his foot encountered a hard object and his ankle rolled. Peter fell to his knees. A wave knocked him sideways into a cluster of floating garden pots. He came up sputtering, grabbing a porch rail and pulling himself into a standing position.

Outside less than five minutes and he was already soaked. At least his flashlight was waterproof.

He recognized the door to Maggie's condo, but when he looked at her living room window, his heart sank.

An enormous log had broken through the wooden board covering the picture window facing east, shattering the glass behind it. He could see it all clearly—the scene before him unfolding like a movie in the dim light of a table lamp. Maggie had started the portable generator she kept high on a sturdy shelf strapped to the wall. Her earthquake preparations were legendary.

The living room was filled with water and debris. As he surveyed the damage to Maggie's place, he realized how lucky he'd been that the boards covering his windows had held.

"Maggie!" he shouted.

No response.

Peter winced and pulled himself up on the windowsill, climbing inside. Shivering from cold and nerves, he cautiously stepped through the window and into the turbid water. It reached his calves as he advanced deeper into the living room.

Inside Maggie's condo, the howl of wind and booming surf gave way to the sounds of Peter's boots sloshing through the house. He could see Maggie's beloved mid-century couch in the dirty water. A Danish bookcase had fallen. Maggie's collection of paperback mystery novels bobbed on the surface.

As he moved toward the kitchen, he spotted something floating in the middle of the hall and froze. Heart pounding, he slowly approached it, a wheezy gasp escaping his throat.

It was Maggie, face down in the water, her long silver hair loose and billowing, like the tendrils of some exotic plant.

"No!" he cried, then slogged toward her. He gently turned her over, his hand sliding beneath her neck.

It was dark in the hall but still light enough for him to see the empty holes where her eyes had been, her mouth stretched into a rictus of terror. Her clothes were shredded, and she had deep lacerations on her face and neck, like she'd been dragged through a field of barbed wire.

In all his years patrolling the beach, he'd never encountered wounds like these. Peter scanned the condo for something that could have done it—like a broken-off bit of fence with exposed nails—but he saw nothing.

It was something else, then. Something in the water. His thoughts returned to the puncture wounds that had killed Matt and the fisherman from San Jose.

Bile rising in his throat, fingers trembling, he inspected Maggie's neck, then her limbs for any signs of puncture wounds. When he didn't find anything, he gingerly lifted what remained of her sweater, revealing pale skin crisscrossed with gashes and scratches but no deep holes ringed in black slime.

Water continued to pour into the living room. He had to get out. But first, he had to do something about Maggie. If he left her there, the water might drag her out to sea. And then he remembered the leash she kept by the kitchen door. She'd lost her black lab a few months back but couldn't bring herself to throw away the leash. Maggie only ever had labs, so the leash was long and sturdy and would do the trick.

Peter lurched into the kitchen, pulling Maggie's body along with him. The filthy water smelled of salt and metal. Behind him, debris bashed into the living room wall with the constant roar of the ocean.

The red leash was where he remembered it, hanging from a hook next to the door. He lashed it around Maggie's waist, hands brushing her cold skin, and looped it through the handle of her old stove.

Maggie bobbed in the water, a corpse bound to a kitchen appliance. It felt as if he'd committed a grave offense, inflicted a terrible indignity on this woman who had been a friend to him and his mother.

It was also a tragic bit of irony. Maggie hated to cook. But he couldn't think of another solution.

Tears stung his eyes as he waded toward the door. When he opened it, a wave nearly knocked him backward. Struggling against the current of water, desperately trying to maintain his footing, Peter managed to steady himself before emerging back out into the violent storm, the thunder of the ocean almost drowning out his thoughts.

Chapter 14

wave height 18.1 ft

Waves pushed against Peter from behind, then the receding water shoved him back. He made his way along the path running in front of the condos but saw nobody else. Several times, he clutched at porch railings to keep from being swept away. Each step forward was a struggle, forcing his limbs into painful protest. When he finally lurched up the steps to the service road connecting the pier to Cortina Bridge, he was met by a river of rushing water.

Holding onto the gate at the end of the staircase for support, Peter peered around the side of the building and immediately understood. The waves were crashing over the pier, transforming the deck into a funnel and channeling water down the service road, with the condos on one side and the San Refugio Hotel & Suites on the other. He'd have to navigate the rush of water gushing across the bridge. The debris-filled creek lapped over the roadbed, flowing under the bridge and out to sea. At any moment, a tree trunk or picnic table or who knew what could come careening over the bridge.

Jesus.

The sounds of the wind and rain were deafening, making it hard to think. The storm pushed against him, relentless and unforgiving. There was no other way but across. The clouds blocked the moon, and it was too dark to see much of anything. He could only hope he'd avoid getting knocked unconscious by something in the roiling water.

Hope was all he had. It was too dark to see anything coming at him until it was too late.

Peter paused. Waves came in sets. Perhaps the current set would taper off soon. Unless he was in between them. Then things would only get worse when the next rolled in. He had to take a chance.

The wind and rain were relentless, and it seemed like an eternity, but eventually, Peter could sense the waves slowing, if only a little bit. Taking a deep breath, he stepped out onto the bridge and immediately felt the surge of water grab hold of him and sweep him along. The creek had risen. He had no control over his movements as he was carried away by the current.

The water rushed around him, dragging him with it along the length of the bridge. He crashed into the concrete wall on the ocean side, then bounced away. Something sharp jabbed his shoulder. A moment later, a large, hard object bashed into his hip. A plastic trash bin spun away in the swirling water. If his reflexes had been faster, Peter could have tried to grab the handle and use it to help him float across.

At the end of the bridge where it dipped to meet Ocean View Drive, he slammed into a mass of debris. Peter felt a sudden stab of pain in his chest, followed by a stinging burn.

A wave of water crashed over his head, and he was pulled under. Moments later, he came up sputtering, disoriented, desperately trying to get his feet under him. If only he could stand, but he'd been spun around and now found himself being carried along in the water, legs stretched out, arms flailing.

Peter tried to remember his training, focus on his breathing, avoid the overwhelming urge to panic.

Then he'd broken through the morass of debris and was being swept down Ocean View Drive, still backward, but at least headed in the right direction.

Peter struggled to keep his head above the surface, when something lit up the water, as bright as a beacon and white like a headlamp. And that's what it was. The headlamp of an electric bicycle tumbling in the waves, and for a moment, Peter saw something swimming alongside it. The rider? No. It couldn't be. A shark? Why not? They lived in the Monterey Bay and were often spotted at the end of the San Refugio Pier. It was probably as disoriented as he was.

Time seemed to slow. The shape was wrong. Too slim, even for a juvenile shark, and no signature fin either. A slightly bulbous head. And it was so dark it was nearly black.

An icy tingle ran up his spine. The damn thing seemed to be staring at him. From off to the right, the trunk of a small tree shot up out of the churning water, spun a few times, then slammed into the thing. Both disappeared into the swirling foam.

Peter managed to dodge the bike as the headlamp whizzed past him and vanished.

Another rush of water swept Peter down Ocean View Drive. He was so focused on keeping his head above the surface, he found himself hurtling past Pancha's Restaurant, powerless to stop. Moments later, he slammed into the steps leading to a small plaza and, beyond it, a bandshell. The stage was several feet above the street and was protected by a concrete wall. Gasping, Peter crawled up the stairs, water tugging at his ankles, until he reached the top. Waves swirled up to the second step but went no higher.

He'd made it. Almost.

Peter would have to get back into the water and fight against the current to get to Carla. He stumbled to the bandshell to get out of the rain—sand and pebbles gritty inside his boots, wet clothing an oppressive weight. His back ached from fighting the current. There was no one around. All was dark above him. The bandshell sat below a steep bluff. There was an apartment building up there, he knew, along with a row of two-story cottages. But he could see not a single light, which meant the power outage had impacted the San Refugio Heights neighborhood too.

With unsteady hands, he unzipped his jacket pocket, pulled out his flashlight, and flicked it on. Peter gave a shaky, giddy laugh when the beam illuminated the concrete benches in front of the bandshell, tumbled together in a heap by the raging sea. At the top step, he trained his flashlight in the direction of the ocean.

The waves were enormous. If the boards protecting the restaurant windows failed…

He needed to be inside and upstairs with Carla before that happened.

Pointing his flashlight at the water flowing toward him, Peter could make out the debris. Wood. Plastic bottles. Cheap patio chairs. No sign of that thing he'd seen in the water. He'd surely imagined it. The muscle relaxants had messed with his head. It was probably just one of those inflatable pool toys shaped like a dolphin they sold at the shops.

Peter pocketed his flashlight, took a deep breath, and waded back into the water. Jesus, it was cold.

Twice, the current knocked him backward, returning him to the steps where he'd started. He reached Pancha's Restaurant on the third attempt, wrapping his arms around a light pole outside to keep from being dragged away as he wondered how to get in. Surely, the door was locked.

The small bathroom window was the best option. The water wasn't high enough to reach it—at least, not yet—and the outside of the building had a facade of rough-hewn sandstone bricks. Several of them protruded far enough to climb on.

Peter launched himself across the sidewalk. He slowly climbed up the wall, the toes of his boots finding a hold between the bricks. Peter pounded the window with his fist...and waited. And waited. No one came. Not surprising. Peter couldn't compete with the noise of the storm.

He'd have to break the window and climb in. After he managed to get to the light pole again, wrapping an arm around the metal column, he dug out his flashlight and shone the beam at the water. It took what seemed like another eternity before he spotted a piece of driftwood close enough for him to grab.

Minutes later, the window shattered, Peter tumbled onto the floor of the men's bathroom in Pancha's Restaurant.

He paused, catching his breath and taking inventory of his aching body. Through his soaked clothes, he couldn't tell if he was bleeding anywhere, but he was certain that jab to the chest had broken the skin.

Peter pulled himself to his feet but fell back against the wall in pain.

And that's when he heard it...

Water rushing somewhere below the restaurant and a creaking sound coming from the floorboards.

Chapter 15

heavy rain

At the sound of Carla's voice, Peter looked up and wiped his eyes with the back of his hand. Was he crying, or was his face just wet from the rain?

Then Lucas was there, hauling Peter to his feet. He was surprised by the sinewy strength of the young man. It hurt to stand, and his chest throbbed where something had jabbed it.

He was on his feet, limping but standing upright, supported by Lucas on one side and Carla on the other.

"You nearly gave me a heart attack, Peter. Where the hell were you?" Carla's voice was a throaty mix of worry and relief.

He felt her hand on his face, her breath warm on his skin.

"Just doing a little body surfing." Peter gave a bitter laugh. He winced. It made his chest hurt.

She squeezed his arm. "Why didn't you come earlier?"

His mind, addled by the muscle relaxants and his adrenaline-fueled escape from his condo, had trouble remembering, but his back didn't forget. The battering he'd taken in the debris-filled water hadn't done him any favors. At least he'd brought his meds with him. They were safe inside a little plastic bottle, tucked away in the zippered pocket of his jacket. He couldn't wait to get out of the heavy, wet clothes.

"I took some muscle relaxers, and they knocked me out."

Carla couldn't hide her surprise. "You fell asleep? In this storm?"

"Yeah. Sure did."

"That's some powerful stuff right there," Lucas said. "My grandpa has back trouble, and he takes them too."

If he had the energy, Peter would have swatted the young man. Instead, he groaned.

Carla chuckled. "All right, old man, let's get you upstairs so you can get out of those wet clothes before your ass starts chapping."

"What happened? Is everything okay?" It was Yuki, calling down from the top of the stairs.

Peter couldn't see her, but he could hear the worry in her voice. He was surprised she was up and around.

"It's Peter," Carla said. "He made it, and he's fine. Mostly."

A beam of bright light came from just inside the stairwell. As they drew closer, he saw it was Eric Chen, holding his camera. The light bobbed toward them.

Eric zoomed in on Peter's face and asked, "What's it like out there?" His gaze was fixed on the viewfinder while he waited for an answer.

Peter stopped and raised his chin. He felt Carla tug his arm, but he saw no point in denying the reporter an interview. "Bad. The high tide hit the pier and the condos, and I got out just in time. Cortina Creek flooded. Ocean View Drive is a river. There's—"

A deafening crash interrupted him.

Eric's camera light swung toward the back wall of the restaurant.

A huge log had smashed through a boarded window, splintering the wood and shattering the glass. Water rushed in, carrying with it a wave of debris. Yuki's screams echoed in the stairwell. Carla grabbed Peter's arm and pulled him toward the stairs, while Lucas moved to Eric's side, frozen, watching in stunned silence.

As they sped toward the stairs, Carla turned and shouted at Lucas and Eric. "Move!"

The raging water filled the room, the air suddenly thick with salty brine. Tables and chairs smashed against the walls, a cacophony of wood and metal, splintering, crashing, and the roar of the victorious ocean that had breached their pathetic defenses.

The walls and floor rumbled and vibrated, sending shivers down Peter's spine.

He'd been so close to being swept away outside, and now, the water was inside and rising fast. After seeing the tree trunk that bashed its way into Maggie's place, he wasn't surprised, but experiencing the destructive power of the surge from inside the restaurant was different. It was like being trapped in an industrial-sized washing machine, without the power to turn it off. Peter felt a jolt of fear. He'd assumed the water couldn't reach the second floor, but what if he'd been wrong?

What if the building couldn't withstand the pounding of the surf and debris?

Lucas was ahead of them, clearing a path through floating chairs and tables. By the time they reached the stairwell, the water was above their knees.

The stairs were long and narrow. Eric Chen climbed atop the bar and recorded their ascent.

The climb—which Peter had done countless times without a second thought—exhausted him. His clothes were soaked and heavy, his feet leaden. He felt every one of his injuries, using the banister to push himself up the steps. Carla's father had built them, and they were too steep to be up to code.

"Just as good as a Stairmaster," Carla liked to joke. But the steps were no joking matter now.

His chest heaved as he made it to the second floor. When he glanced back, he saw the water lapping at the lower steps.

Peter stood on the landing, one hand against the wall for support, as Carla pulled off his jacket. Yuki appeared with a bucket and set it down at his feet. He stared at it in confusion. Did she think he was about to be sick? And then he understood. The women meant for him to strip off his wet clothes before entering.

Lucas patted his shoulder, then disappeared inside. Yuki returned with a towel and handed it to Carla before turning on her heel, quietly closing the door behind her. Even in her grief, Yuki was considerate.

Mindful of Eric Chen behind him, Peter turned, neck aching. The young reporter was out of sight, no doubt still preoccupied with the churning water below.

The wet clothes clung to his body like a second skin, weighing him down. He was grateful for Carla's help peeling away the sodden layers.

When his socks, sneakers, and even his briefs were in the bucket, the towel wrapped around his waist, they went inside.

There was no sign of Yuki. She'd probably retreated to the guestroom. Lucas was there, regarding him somberly. Peter lurched past him and headed straight for Carla's small bathroom.

"The gas is still working, so how about you take a quick shower?"

She sat on the toilet seat, holding the flashlight as Peter rinsed off the grime and salt.

When he was done, he staggered to the bed and sank onto the soft mattress with a groan. The weak light of an electric lantern on the nightstand cast shadows on the walls. Carla disappeared into the closet and came out, holding the clothes he kept at her place.

His back spasmed, and he winced. Carla pushed herself between his knees and gingerly dried his hair with a small towel.

"*Madre mia*," she murmured. "You're a mess."

Carla tsked when she inventoried his wounds, fingers gently probing his scalp, the tender skin on his face where he'd scraped or bruised it. Her eyes snapped open when she noticed the gash on the right side of his chest.

"Oh my God, is that…" Her words faltered, strangled by her growing alarm.

Peter stared down at his ripped flesh.

He was relieved to see irregular edges. The wound was at least five inches long, mean and narrow. Bad, but no gaping hole ringed with black. If it had been, he'd probably be dead by now. Whatever had scratched him had been an ordinary bit of debris, like a bit of metal railing torn from the pier.

Peter reached for Carla's hand and kissed it. It was dry and warm. "No, no, it's not that. It's bad, but it's fine. There was a bunch of crap in the water. That's all."

She rummaged through a small wicker basket of first aid supplies. "When was the last time you had a tetanus shot?"

He thought for a moment. "Three years ago. It'll be fine."

"This needs stitches. I've got some butterfly bandages. It's not great, but…"

Peter nervously glanced at the door before speaking. He felt a sudden and intense urge to tell Carla what happened back at the San Refugio Ocean Condos.

"Maggie's dead."

Carla gasped softly. "Oh no. What happened?"

"I don't know." Peter wanted her to know—he really did—but when he registered her anxious expression, he couldn't bring himself to tell her about Maggie's missing eyes.

Chapter 16

strong winds

The group gathered in Carla's living room. Yuki perched on the edge of an easy chair, back straight, hands folded in her lap. Lucas and Eric sat on the floor, leaning against the wall, legs stretched out. Eric clutched his camera on his lap. Peter rested on the couch next to Carla, gripping her hand. The entryway door was open, and waves sloshed down below. An enormous log bumped into the walls. More waves crashed inside, bringing with them more debris.

The last time Lucas checked, several trash bins, a cooler, and a patio umbrella had washed into the dining room through the shattered back windows. The restaurant was now almost completely open to the raging surf.

How long could the building stand?

Carla had offered everyone a beer, but Peter refused. He needed a clear head, and it wasn't clear enough to suit him. Thoughts and reactions weren't coming fast enough after the double dose of pain pills he'd taken. His back was bruised and sore from his adventure across Cortina Bridge and down Ocean View Drive, but at least it hadn't gone out completely.

Eric was first to break the uneasy silence. "Do you think we're safe up here?" The camera wasn't pointed at Peter, but the question was directed at him all the same.

Peter cleared his throat. "We're fourteen feet off the ground. The water will eventually recede. What worries me is that all that debris might start bringing down the front wall and wash out to Ocean View Drive."

"Should we try to open the front door?" Lucas said, voice tentative. "You know. Give the water an easy way out?"

Carla's reaction was explosive. "No. Absolutely not. The only way you can get to the front door is through that debris. You'll be smashed to bits."

Lucas held up his hands. "Okay, okay. I was just asking."

Carla looked away, biting her lip. Peter squeezed her leg.

"What do we do, then?" Eric asked.

Peter sighed. He'd always had a bias toward action. It had served him well as a park ranger. But now, he felt helpless. There was nothing he could do, no action he could take, to get them to safety. It was arguable they should have evacuated when they could, but the weather forecast hadn't called for it. The wrong forecast, it turned out.

It was unlikely the water would reach them on the second floor, but it was still scary sitting on top of a storm surge.

Peter turned to Carla. Her dark eyes were pools of anxiety.

"Who else is around? Ken?"

She nodded. "Yeah. We should check on him. He said he wanted to talk to you. Don't ask me about what because he wouldn't say. The women in the vacation rental stayed. And Amalia. I saw her lights when I was outside earlier. She must have the generator going."

Peter shifted on the couch. It was hard to get comfortable with the gash in his chest. The butterfly bandages weren't up to the task, and he could feel the flesh pulling with each movement, a burning, searing pain that made him grit his teeth. His right hand was swollen, the knuckles scraped raw.

"I think the safest choice is to stay where we are," he finally said. "And wait it out."

Lucas scrambled to his feet. "I can make quesadillas."

Carla snorted.

Yuki kicked her foot. "Yes, Carla. The boys are probably hungry. Peter included."

Eric's hand shot up. "I'm down. I'm starving. I didn't get to finish my burrito."

The two young men disappeared into the kitchen.

Carla threw up her hands. "Why are they still here?" she hissed. "Why don't they go back to Lucas's place?"

Peter took a deep breath and exhaled slowly. "Because they're probably freaked out and trying not to show it. Come on."

Yuki frowned at Carla. "They know Peter was the go-to authority on the beach, and they feel safer with him around. I know I do."

Peter's throat tightened. He felt helpless and more than a bit useless. Peter reached across Carla and patted Yuki's hand. She pressed hers to her mouth, rose, and hurried to her room. Just before she closed the door, a sob escaped her throat.

"She didn't want to stay with family or something?" Peter asked. It occurred to him, for all the time he'd known the Harmons, he knew little about their personal lives.

Carla shook her head. "She doesn't really have any family. Her parents are dead, and she's an only child. They couldn't have kids. So, no."

"Jesus." Peter couldn't imagine being that alone in the world. As much as his brother sometimes annoyed him, he couldn't picture life without him or his sister-in-law and nephews.

Carla wasn't much better off—no siblings, just some cousins, and her only child dead.

A loud creaking interrupted his thoughts. It was coming from down below. Peter and Carla exchanged looks, then slowly rose to their feet. Eric stepped into the living room, eyebrows raised.

"What's that noise?" he asked.

Peter shook his head. "I don't know."

"Whatever it is, it doesn't sound good," Carla replied grimly.

They hurried toward the stairwell. The creaking continued, growing louder with every step they descended. Eric was the last in line with his camera, the light bouncing off the walls of the narrow staircase, eventually settling on the churning water. Peter could feel Carla's hands on his shoulders.

It sounded like something was trying to break through the floorboards.

The light jerked upward, and from behind him, Eric gasped. "Did you see that?"

The light from Eric's camera panned wildly from one side of the flooded dining room to the other. The uncontrolled movement hurt Peter's eyes.

As the light swept across the room, Peter saw the flash of a long dark shape gliding beneath the surface before it vanished. He held his breath, heart pounding as he scanned the murky water.

There it was again, behind a trash bin—a shadowy form.

Peter had the fleeting impression it was trying to hide. And then it was gone, lost among the churn of logs, branches, and floating chairs.

A deafening boom shattered the air. Water exploded upward with such force, planks of wood were sent flying, like missiles into the air.

The waves under the restaurant had broken through the floor.

Peter instinctively threw himself backward, colliding with Carla as the spray of seawater narrowly missed them. There was an ear-splitting shriek when one side of the bar tilted upward, like an invisible hand pushed it from below.

The chaos seemed to go on forever. Then gradually, the creaking and groaning of erupting wood stopped, and all he could hear was the continuous roar of the incoming tide. The murky waters rushed toward the center of the room, where the worst of the destruction seemed concentrated. Moments later, another rush of seawater came shooting up.

When Eric squeezed in next to him for a better angle, Peter took his arm and focused the light on the middle of the room. He saw only floor joists and debris-filled water swirling there.

The floor was gone and, with it, their path to the exit.

Chapter 17

rainfall 1.4 inches per hour

Eric dashed up the steps and into the apartment. Carla shoved her shoulder under Peter's arm, trying to support him while slowly making their way up the stairs. His fall backward had strained his back, and he winced every time he lifted his foot.

When they finally shuffled into the living room, Eric's camera sat on the coffee table.

Carla paused, glancing around. "Where's Eric?"

"He went to my place to get his backpack," Lucas said. "His laptop is in there. He says he saw something swimming around in the water and thinks he got it on video."

Carla frowned. "Everything in the restaurant is swimming around. What do you mean by 'something'?"

"I don't know." Lucas shrugged.

Beside her, she felt Peter stiffen.

Yuki was back, perched on the green velvet chair. "What happened? What was all that noise?"

"The surf took out the floorboards," Peter said. "If it happened here, it probably happened to your place and Bigg's Bar too."

Carla felt a chill run up her arms. She'd never given much thought to the building beneath her feet. All three businesses sat atop wooden pilings, allowing water to collect below during high tide. It was a piece of driftwood caught under Ken's place that had kept her awake just the night before, clattering against the structure.

The patio door slid open, and a gust of wind and rain blew inside. Eric put his backpack on the floor and pulled out a silver laptop. They watched him remove a small chip from the camera, fitting it into a slot on his laptop.

Beside her, Peter fidgeted. When she glanced up at him, his eyelid was twitching.

"What's going on?" she asked. "What's he talking about?"

Peter bit his lip. "I think I saw it too."

"Could someone please explain what's going on?" Yuki sounded nervous.

Eric glanced up, his face set in concentration. "There was something swimming around in the water. Something alive." His fingers danced across the keyboard. "We'll see if I got it or not."

Yuki and Lucas stood behind Eric and stared at the screen.

Carla nudged Peter. "Did you see it?"

He dipped his head, slipping his hands into the pocket of his hoodie. Peter seemed uncharacteristically edgy.

"What did you see?" she persisted. "A shark?"

Peter didn't answer, captivated by the flickering laptop screen as Eric sped through the video.

Eric's finger jabbed at a key. "There!" he cried, pointing excitedly.

They leaned in, heads bent, breaths drawn. Then she saw it. Something surfaced for a moment, its long, thick, oddly shaped body a strange shade of oily black. The creature paused, as if suddenly aware it was being watched.

It resembled nothing she'd seen at the Monterey Bay Aquarium, and she'd spent a lot of time there when Jacob was a little boy. They'd gone so often, she'd splurged on a season pass.

Yuki clapped a hand over her mouth. "Is that…a face?"

"Kind of," Lucas said, squinting at the screen.

Eric glanced up at Peter. "You ever seen that before?"

"No." Peter's voice was troubled, distant.

Carla stepped closer for a better look, swallowing. It had a vaguely human form, with a dome-like head, two small round eyes, a protrusion that passed for a nose, and a small frowning mouth.

"It's freaky as fuck," Lucas said.

Peter patted the young man's shoulder. "You got that right."

"Why's it all lit up like that?" Yuki stared at the screen.

"Bioluminescence?" Carla ventured.

Eric frowned. "Could be. Some fish have light-producing organs. Anglerfish have them, but the lights dangle from a rod that sticks out of its head. That sort of looks like a barreleye, but they're small. Maybe six or eight inches. This is too big. *Way* too big."

Carla sniffed. "You sure know a lot about fish."

Eric kept staring at the screen. "My mom's a marine biologist at one of the labs at Moss Landing, so I guess it was inevitable."

"How big are the sharks around here?" Carla's voice betrayed her anxiety. From what she could tell, the thing swimming around downstairs wasn't equipped with a menacing row of razor-sharp teeth. But maybe its mouth was on the underside, and they couldn't see it.

Peter sat back in his chair. "That's too small for a great white. Males are around twelve feet. The females can get up to sixteen feet."

"It's definitely not a shark," Eric said.

Carla's hair had escaped its ponytail. She pushed it back from her face. "Okay. Then what *is* that thing in my restaurant? You said your mom is a marine biologist? Can you send her a picture?"

Peter's hand tightened on Carla's shoulder. "We don't have a signal, remember?" He cleared his throat. "I might have seen that thing before."

Carla spun around to stare at Peter. "You saw that? Where?"

"On my way here," Peter replied. "In the water. Just for a second. I thought it was maybe one of the dolphin float toys they sell around here."

"Was it the same…fish?" she asked, voice rising.

"I'm not sure how many there are. It could be the same one."

"If there's one, there are probably more," Lucas added.

Carla swallowed, dread settling into her stomach. First the storm hitting much harder than the city forecast. Then logs crashing through the dining room windows, surf tearing up the floorboards. The whole building could come down, with them in it.

And now this. This not-a-barreleye, not-a-shark…thing.

Carla hoped the building held. Whatever it was, the last thing she wanted was to encounter it in the water. For all they knew, it was the same fish that had killed Matt and the man from San Jose.

She quickly moved to close and lock the apartment door. Just in case.

Chapter 18

winds gusting to 54 mph
wave height 18.2 ft

Carla went into the bathroom. Of course, she'd started her period, tonight of all nights. It had stopped giving notice to her body. No more cramps. No more horrible backaches. Not even a headache or bad mood to signal it was coming. It just showed up, an uninvited guest. She reached under the sink for a tampon. When she was finished washing her hands—at least they still had water—she ran a comb through her hair and tied it back into a low ponytail. Her teeth felt mossy, so she quickly brushed. She was turning around when she noticed the wall opposite the sink.

The crack running up the plaster was new.

She looked around and counted three more. Two in the shower stall on the outer wall. One behind the toilet.

A quick walk around the apartment revealed cracks in tile grout and nail heads coming out of drywall, too many to count.

Peter looked up from Eric's laptop. Everyone had moved to the kitchen table, obsessively studying the six-second video frame by frame. They'd concluded the creature in the water didn't have fins and were now attempting to estimate its size.

"What's up?" Peter said absently.

Carla took a deep breath, trying to calm the rising anxiety threatening to overwhelm her, and pointed at the wall facing the ocean. Even with the window closed, she could hear the raging sea's continued onslaught on her restaurant.

A diagonal crack, starting just inches above the baseboard, climbed the wall all the way to the ceiling—etched in stark contrast to the coastal white paint Yuki had helped her choose.

"That wasn't there before," Peter said, voice faint.

Carla pressed a hand against her chest. Her heart was pounding so hard, it felt like a caged animal was in there, trying to escape.

"There are cracks all over the apartment." She swallowed. "When the floor came up, it might have messed up the foundation or the load-bearing walls."

Yuki sat back in her chair, blinking. "Didn't you say your dad built the apartment?"

"Yeah. I was a kid when he did it. My uncles helped." Carla hesitated. "It's not built to code. None of it is. They built it under the radar. They said it would never pass inspection."

Peter's mouth opened, then closed. "Did they say anything about what might happen if there was ever an earthquake?"

Carla felt lightheaded, dizzy, like the room was spinning. "They said it could be bad, but I mean, we had that big earthquake when I was a kid, and the place was fine. My uncles talked about shear walls and cross-braces, but there's no way my dad could afford to do all that."

Peter was staring at a crack in the drywall like he expected it to talk. "How about Bigg's places? Do you think they're up to code?"

Carla bit the inside of her cheek so hard she winced. "I don't know. We've never talked about it."

Peter turned to Yuki, who shook her head. "I have no idea."

"Are you saying what I think you're saying?" Eric asked, sitting back in his chair.

Peter got up and began to pace. "If the surf destabilized the load-bearing walls, it's possible the building we're in could collapse, and if that's the case, we need to get out of here before it does."

"How?" Carla's mouth dried up. "We're surrounded by water! Look what happened to you, just trying to cross the bridge, and you're an expert swimmer."

"I surf, so I'm good in the water," Eric said.

"If I had to, I'd probably be fine," Lucas added. He pointed at the laptop screen. "But doesn't that mean going through the restaurant? What about that thing? We don't know if it's dangerous or—"

Yuki cleared her throat. "I'll say it if no one else wants to. That thing could be what killed my husband and that other man too." She shifted in her chair and stared at Eric. "You said in your story that people were talking about a 'deadly creature.' Well, we could be looking at it."

Carla's eyebrows knitted together. She recalled her conversation earlier that evening with the reporter. "Eric, you said you had a source who told you about a creature. A marine scientist who looked at the photos. So, if you know something useful, now's the time to tell us."

Eric pinched his bottom lip and stared blankly at the screen. Finally, he sighed. "It's my mom. She's the marine scientist."

Lucas snorted. "Whoa. His mommy is his top-secret source."

Carla glanced at Lucas in surprise. His resentful tone was unexpected. She'd pegged him as sweet and rather shy, but there was an edge to him that caught her off guard. And by the looks of it, Eric too. He winced.

"Can you please tell us a little more about what your mom said?" Yuki put a shaky hand to her head.

Peter brought his fist down on the table, and they all jumped. "No 'please' about it. You need to tell us exactly what she said because we need to know what we're dealing with if…if…" He stopped and shook his head. "I can't believe this is happening. Any of it."

Carla went over to him and squeezed his shoulder. She could feel a giant knot of tension under her fingers. "Okay, okay. First things first. Eric, you tell us what you know, and then we need to try and figure out the condition of the places on both sides of us. Right? Maybe we can go to Lucas's place and hang out until this is over. Or if that's bad, we can go to Bigg's."

"No, we can't," Yuki said. "Your balcony doesn't connect to Ken's."

Carla shrugged. "There's a ledge. I've done it plenty of times." Before anyone could respond, she turned to Eric and crossed her arms in front of her chest. "Let's hear it."

Eric gave a defeated sigh. "Seriously, I don't know much more than I've already said. At least, nothing that's helpful. As soon as she heard about the tourist in the boat, she and some of the other biologists decided to come over and look for it. They're going to use submersibles." He got up and refilled his water glass at the tap.

Carla and Peter exchanged glances. Something the reporter had said nagged at her. He had the same evasive expression her son used to get when he didn't want to tell her the whole truth.

98

Her eyes widened. "Eric. You make it sound like your mother's not surprised there's something nasty swimming around in the bay."

Eric set down his glass and rolled his neck. "It's just an old story."

Peter barked out a laugh. "No way. Not *that* story."

"She was there," Eric said stubbornly. "She saw it."

Peter leaned forward. "Wait. That was your mom?"

"It was," Eric admitted. "It's not something she likes talking about. She's going to flip out when she sees my video. Maybe her bosses will finally believe her."

Carla stole a glance at Yuki and Lucas, their faces scrunched in bewilderment.

She stomped a foot. "Peter. Eric. Can one of you clue us in, please? We have no idea what the hell you're talking about."

"My mom is part of a group that studies ocean-warming effects on species coming in and out of Monterey Bay," Eric said. "Endangered species, new invasive species, migration patterns, whatever. They're changing all the time. A few years ago, the lab got this new underwater robot that can go down really deep and collect DNA samples. They launch it off a boat. My mom and her partner were monitoring the live video stream from the ship, and they saw something big about two miles down. That's really, really deep. At first, they thought it was some sort of eel, but it was fast. They'd never seen anything like it before." He rubbed the side of his face. "So, this is where it gets weird, and you need to believe me when I say my mom isn't the type of person to exaggerate, or lie, or anything like that." The reporter's cheeks flushed. "They said it almost looked human."

Carla laughed. "You mean, like a mermaid? Are you kidding me?"

"Did you hear me say that word?" Eric snapped. "Because I don't remember using it. I never use it."

Peter was shaking his head. "No. The word is 'humanoid.'" He glanced over at Eric, who was leaning against the counter, arms folded across his chest.

Eric's eyes darkened. "That's pretty much it. They lost the signal. The camera failed, and then the submersible imploded. My mom's partner forgot to record the video feed, so it was just the two of them, telling their boss what they saw. But then everybody started joking about it. My mom wishes they'd never said anything."

There was a moment of stunned silence before Yuki cleared her throat. When she spoke, her voice was high and shrill. "I'm no expert, and no one is asking my opinion, but…" She paused long enough to point a trembling finger at the computer screen. "That thing looks humanoid to me. Anyone else?"

"Oh yeah," Lucas said, then grimaced.

Peter released Carla's hand and rubbed his face. "Okay, then. If our guest down below is the same one Eric's mom saw down in the deep, then it survived a couple years without being detected. I think it's safe to assume the storm brought it ashore."

Lucas leaned forward and set his elbows on the table. "But why would it attack people now? It's been down there for years, right?"

"Maybe the storm agitated it," Peter suggested. "Or maybe it becomes aggressive as it gets older."

Chapter 19

heavy rain
52°

Everyone was staring at Peter like he knew what to do. He felt like he *should* know. He'd spent a career solving other people's problems. But nothing about working for the State Parks Department had prepared him for this.

Did the cracks in the walls mean the apartment was about to pancake on top of the flooded restaurant below? The apartment shared common walls with its neighbors. If those buildings weren't damaged, would they keep Carla's apartment from collapsing, or would they all come down at once?

Scarier still was that thing swimming below, which could be the same sea creature that had killed two men, including his friend, Matt. Was the thing still there? The surf could have washed it out by now.

Though he couldn't be absolutely sure, whatever it was seemed to have registered their presence. If it was a predator, it was probably circling, waiting for an easy meal to literally drop in its lap.

Peter knew one thing—you don't make progress by sitting around. He needed more information. That simple acknowledgment broke through his paralysis.

Peter turned to Lucas. "Why don't you run over to your place and check the walls for damage. Look carefully and take pictures if you find any."

"I can do that," Lucas replied eagerly. He shot to his feet, snatching his jacket from the back of his chair, and left.

Peter heard the sliding door in the living room open, then shut again. "We need to see what's going on at Ken's place," he said, frowning as he remembered the balconies didn't connect.

"And check on Ken too," Carla said. "To tell you the truth, I'm a little worried about him, with his diabetes and all. I'll go."

Peter shook his head. "There's no railing on that ledge. It's wet and slippery. You can fall."

"It's fine. That ledge sticks out a good two and a half feet, and it's made of rough stucco, so it's pretty grippy."

Peter imagined losing his footing and toppling into the waves below. The year before, he'd fallen from a ladder at home. His confidence had taken a hit.

His brother's merciless teasing hadn't helped either. Bro. Maybe you need to take one of those classes for seniors, where they help with balance and mobility.

He was being ridiculous. Peter had never had trouble with heights while he was working. Retirement was turning him into a nervous nelly. And he wasn't about to let Carla go into the storm alone and deal with Ken all by herself. He pushed himself to his feet.

Carla was already putting on her jacket. He told Yuki and Eric to stay put until they returned.

Eric gave a grim laugh. "I guess I won't run downstairs and make a margarita, then."

Carla insisted on going first, climbing over the balcony railing and onto the overhang, one hand gripping a flashlight. She sidestepped quickly across the ledge, then swung a leg over the railing and stood on Ken's balcony.

She aimed the beam of light at the jutting shelf of stucco at his feet. "Just stay close to the wall and look at me," she said.

The roar of the ocean added to his disorientation. Jesus. What had happened to the big, strong lifeguard? He felt like a wimp. What the hell was wrong with him? Peter gritted his teeth and clambered over the railing, back twinging in protest, then put one foot in front of the other. When he reached Ken's balcony, he let go a quiet sigh of relief.

Carla was pounding her fist against the sliding glass door. When she got no response, she tried the handle, and the glass door slid open.

They stepped inside. Three electric lanterns lit the room. Ken was crashed out on the couch, mouth open.

Carla threw off her jacket and rushed to his side. "Ken?" She gave him a little shake. "Wake up, Ken. It's me, Carla."

Peter looked around. The place was even more cluttered than he remembered. Ken's decorating taste ran to kitschy beach decor. A wooden ship's wheel hung above the couch, next to a fishermen's net and a brass plaque that read: "Captain."

When Peter turned back to Ken, his eyes were fluttering open. Carla crouched next to him, eyebrows drawn together.

"Ken. Are you okay? Did you take your insulin?"

Ken struggled to keep his eyes open. "It got out." His voice was faint, weak. His eyes closed.

Carla shot a puzzled look at Peter, then leaned in closer to Ken. "What got out, Ken?"

"I captured it. But it got out." His eyes closed. "Tell Yuki I'm sorry."

A cold, hard knot formed in Peter's chest. "What's he talking about?"

He crossed over to the couch and stared down at Ken. The man's face was waxy and covered with sweat, his eyes unfocused.

Carla crossed the room to the counter separating the living area from the small, old-fashioned kitchen. She held up a small vial and a disposable needle with a bright orange cap. "I'll bet he skipped a dose." A moment later, she groaned and pointed at a bottle of scotch. It was nearly empty. "Oh my God. I think we can guess what happened here. We need to test his blood. There's got to be a glucose meter around here somewhere."

Peter watched Carla search frantically for the device. "Do you even know how to use it?"

"My dad was diabetic, so yeah, I can probably figure it out." She turned her attention to the drawers, then the cupboards.

When Peter returned his attention to Ken, the man's body had gone limp. A chill swept over Peter, and he placed two fingers against Ken's neck, feeling a weak, slow pulse.

"Ken!" Peter shook Ken's arm. He glanced over at Carla with wide eyes. "He's unconscious." His voice was hoarse.

Carla stopped her search and turned slowly, face drained of color. She crossed the room and came to stand beside Peter. "Oh no," she murmured. "This isn't good." She leaned down and placed a hand against Ken's forehead. "I think he's gone into a diabetic coma. That's what happened to my dad before he died."

Peter stared at Ken's still body for several moments before finally standing up and stepping away from the couch. His throat tightened with unexpected emotion, but no sound came out. All he could do was continue staring helplessly at Ken's motionless body.

"I don't see how he can make it."

Carla leaned against him with a sigh. "This is one fucked-up night."

Peter nodded absently. "What the hell was Ken talking about? About capturing something? And apologizing to Yuki?"

"I'm not sure." Carla sounded uneasy. "Earlier tonight, he said he wanted to talk to you. He was panicked."

"And he didn't say what it was about?"

"No. But he was acting funny. Maybe he was already having blood sugar problems." She tugged at his hand. "Peter, we need to get moving."

A groan came from below the apartment, the sound of wet timbers rubbing together.

Their eyes met. The waves and debris were taking a toll on the building.

With renewed urgency, they searched for damage. They had to peer behind fishing nets, wooden signboards, and posters, but they found it. There were cracks in the bedroom walls and in the entryway leading downstairs. The steep staircase led to a vestibule in Harmon's Fish Restaurant, with a door out to the deck in back.

Ken had to cross the dining room to go out the front door, but he could slip out the back and come and go in private. Doors to his apartment and at the bottom of the staircase prevented drunk tourists looking for the bathroom from stumbling into his apartment instead.

They descended the stairs cautiously, Peter taking the lead. It was as noisy as if they'd been standing on the San Refugio Pier, the storm raging around them.

The door at the bottom of the stairs was open. Churning water covered the first couple of steps, mirroring the situation at Carla's place. Hanging onto the railing, Carla clutching the back of his jacket, Peter peered out the door and around the corner.

The restaurant kitchen was gone. The back of Harmon's Fish Restaurant was completely open to the beach and the invading waves.

"Jesus," Peter muttered.

Carla squeezed in next to him and shone the flashlight around the cavernous room. The fancy modern upholstered chairs Yuki had recently purchased bobbed in the water. The expensive textured wallpaper from San Francisco was ruined. The waves had carried in a mass of debris. There was so much more of it in Harmon's, it was impossible to see anything but a churning mix of logs, branches, chairs, tables, ice buckets, and a fake palm tree that had once graced the entrance.

"Do you see anything in the water?" Peter shouted over the din of debris crashing against the walls.

"No, but anything could be in there, and we wouldn't know. Can you tell if the floor is still intact?"

Peter shrugged. "I think so. Doesn't really matter, though. The front door is at the other end of the restaurant. There's no way we can reach it from here. At least, not in one piece."

They retreated upstairs.

Carla's face was pale in the lantern light. Peter could tell she was trying hard not to look at Ken but not succeeding.

"I wonder what Ken was talking about, capturing something or other. Must have been pretty important if he couldn't wait until after the storm to tell us about it."

Carla's mouth opened, then closed, an incredulous look coming to her face. She crossed to the coffee table in two determined strides and snatched up a cell phone from the cluttered surface. It had belonged to Ken. Peter would recognize the red, white, and blue case with the bald eagle anywhere.

She stared at the screen. "Maybe he has pictures of whatever he was talking about."

"Yeah, but we don't have his phone password."

Carla shifted, then grimaced. "We don't need it. We just need to put his finger on the screen." She held out the phone.

Peter swallowed. She was serious. And she was right. He took the phone and, suppressing a shudder, positioned the comatose man's finger against the glass. The home screen came to life. It was as cluttered as Ken's apartment.

He checked the photos as Carla's hand drifted to his shoulder.

They spotted the picture at the same time. A closeup of something in a large steel vat in the storage room at the back of Bigg's Bar.

Peter felt the hairs lift on the back of his neck.

Carla's hand twitched on his shoulder. "What the hell is that?"

Chapter 20

wave height 17.1 ft

Yuki was speechless when she heard about Ken. Lucas flung himself back in his chair, eyes reddening. Peter gazed at him with a heavy heart.

With his dark curls and large brown eyes, Lucas looked younger than his years. Ken had been generous to him, offering affordable rent that allowed Lucas to live closer to campus and avoid the brutal commute from Salinas. He'd even loaned Lucas an old junker he'd had in storage for years so Lucas could go back and forth to school. Unless a miracle happened, Lucas would lose a man who'd made a difference in his life.

Ken had divorced ages ago and had a son in Texas. Sometimes, Ken joked that when he died, the money from his business and rental properties would be enough for his son to buy an entire town in the Lone Star State.

Carla stared at Lucas as if trying to make up her mind about something. Then, to Peter's amazement, she wrapped her arms around the young man's shoulders. A bit awkwardly, Peter noticed, but when Lucas went limp and leaned his head against her arm, tears welled up in Carla's eyes.

Eric got up and made hot tea. At least the gas was still working.

There was no avoiding what needed to happen next.

Peter pulled out Ken's phone, found the photo, and set it on the table.

Yuki, Eric, and Lucas leaned forward, eyes widening.

"Ken took a picture of…that. He said he'd captured it and that it escaped." He paused.

Carla scooted her chair a little closer to Yuki.

"Look." Eric pointed at the tentacle coiled under the creature's underbelly. "It's got a stinger."

Peter dipped his head. "It does." An electric tingle sparked along his spine.

Yuki gave a little cry and slumped against Carla.

Lucas looked up. His eyes were still red. "Just to make sure I'm following, you think that's the 'unidentified species' Eric's mom was talking about that killed Mr. Harmon and the man from San Jose? That stinger doesn't look long enough."

"It's hard to tell," Eric said, voice grim. "It's coiled up, but I'm betting it's hella long when it unravels."

Yuki shifted in her seat to face Peter. "Have you ever seen anything like it before?"

"No," he admitted. His chest felt heavy, like he was wearing one of those weighted vests he used to wear for strength training. The truth was, the thing in the photo scared the hell out of him. It had a strange muscular body, segmented in a way that suggested a human shape, with the slightly iridescent color of a black pearl. And then there was that head.

"It has a face too," Yuki said, voice rising.

Peter sighed. "Yeah.'"

"It could just be an illusion," Eric noted. "Did you see that viral video that some tourist took in China? Everybody said it was a carp with a human face, but it was just some weird markings on the top of its head." He shrugged. "That could be what we're looking at."

"Are there any videos of that thing?" Carla asked.

Peter shook his head. "Just that one photo."

Which suggested Ken hadn't wanted to stay around long enough to shoot a video. The angle and quality of the picture also suggested it was taken in a hurry, maybe while Ken was moving.

Carla exhaled loudly. "Guess this is what Ken meant when he said he'd prove scientists had created a hybrid. What I'd like to know is how and where Ken caught it and how he managed to get it in that tank."

"The only person who can answer that is in a coma. Or by now, maybe worse." Peter sighed.

Eric snorted dismissively. "Did he seriously think my mom was capable of creating something like that? It's not even possible."

"Not your mom specifically." Peter shook his head. "Ken had some crazy ideas."

Yuki gave Eric's arm a light tap. "You know, Eric, parents don't always tell their children everything."

Eric sat back, stung.

"Think about it. Did your mother ever say anything about a special project she was working on? Was she working extra hours?"

"No, but I don't see her that much. I work nights…and weekends. And we don't live in the same house anymore. Not exactly anyway." He paused, a sheepish expression coming to his face. "I live in a studio above the garage. The TV station doesn't pay enough for me to get an apartment on my own."

"There's that privilege again," Lucas muttered.

Eric shot him a dark look but said nothing.

Peter held up a hand. "Okay. Some stuff is just going to have to remain a mystery for a while, but we do know this thing has a venomous stinger, and it escaped. Hopefully, it was so scared, it swam away as fast as possible."

Carla lifted her eyebrows. "Are fish that smart?"

"My mom says they're smarter than we think," Eric said.

"Octopus are," Lucas added. "I watched a documentary about them."

Eric sniffed. "I'm pretty sure that's not an octopus."

Carla rapped her knuckles on the table. "What if, instead of swimming away, it's downstairs, hanging out with its friend?"

"That stinger freaks me out." Lucas shivered. "It's…weapons grade."

Eric cleared his throat. "Speaking of weapons. Do we have any? If we're ever gonna get out of here, we may need some protection."

"Let me check my arsenal and see what I have in stock." Carla tipped her chair back, opened a drawer, pretended to peer inside it, and then slammed it shut. "Nope, fresh out."

She turned to Lucas.

"How about you? You packing over at your place?"

Lucas bristled. "You think I'm a gangbanger now?"

Carla rolled her eyes. "Of course not. Keep your *chonies* on."

To Peter's surprise, Lucas relaxed and grinned. *Chonies* was one of Carla's favorite words—"panties" in Spanish.

Carla blinked, mouth opening slightly. "Wait, didn't Ken talk about having a couple of guns?"

Lucas pushed his shoulders back and jumped to his feet. "He did. All the time. I'll go look."

Before anyone could object, he was out the door.

Chapter 21

blowing rain

The glass door slid open, letting in a blast of cold air, rain, and a drenched Lucas. Carla watched him pull two handguns from the deep pockets of his jacket and set them down on the coffee table.

Peter bent over, frowning at the guns. "That's all he had?"

"That I could find," Lucas said, voice tinged with disappointment. "They were in his nightstand. I thought maybe he had a safe hidden behind the big ship painting, but he didn't."

"No. This is great," Peter replied, picking up the closest firearm. "Two guns are better than none."

Carla leaned against him. God, she was tired. What time was it anyway? She glanced at her phone. Just after 2:00 a.m. "What are they?"

"Two nine millimeters, one with an extra-large magazine."

"Aren't those magazines illegal here?" Yuki said, staring intently at the gun in Peter's hand.

"Yes, but I can guess where he got it. His son from Texas probably hand-delivered it on one of his visits." Peter paused. "Can't say I object to having it now. Considering. Anyone beside me know how to shoot?"

Lucas shook his head. Eric did too.

Yuki put a shaky hand to her head. "I do."

Carla turned to her friend in surprise. "You do? Since when?"

"My dad taught me," Yuki replied, reaching for one of the handguns.

"Okay." Carla watched Yuki inspect the gun. "So now that you two are locked and loaded, now what?"

The plan was simple. Go downstairs, see if there were any strange visitors swimming around in the restaurant, and if not, figure out how to get out of the building before it collapsed.

Peter, armed with the large magazine, would go first, followed by Yuki, who had strict instructions not to accidentally blow his head off. He wanted everyone else to stay in Carla's apartment, but Eric insisted on filming, and there was no way Carla would sit still, twiddling her thumbs. And because Carla was going, Lucas had to go too.

Peter aimed his flashlight at the bottom of the steps. Waves continued to crash in through the back wall, and the enormous log was still there, along with even more debris.

"How long does high tide last?" Lucas asked.

Peter's steps slowed when he neared the bottom of the staircase. "The peak just lasts a few minutes, but it can take hours for the water level to drop back down. It was high tide about an hour ago, so it'll be a while yet." He motioned for Lucas to stand behind him. "Okay. You move that light across the water, and we'll see what we can see. If anything comes at us, I'll shoot it."

Carla couldn't hear much besides the whooshing of blood in her ears. There was so much junk in the water, it—or they—could be hiding anywhere. Yuki stood on the step below her, shoulders up around her ears, the gun clutched in one hand. Her tense stance didn't inspire much confidence, but Yuki had said she knew what she was doing. Carla wasn't sure shooting a gun worked like riding a bike, but what did she know? She'd never held a gun in her life.

"I'm rolling," Eric announced from the rear.

"This is not a movie," Carla snapped.

"Action!" Lucas snickered and swung the beam of his flashlight from one end of the restaurant to the other. The debris rose and fell like a living thing.

The gun in Peter's hand followed the light. "Can we be quiet so I can focus, please?"

"Sorry," Carla whispered. God, she was so tense, her shoulders felt like they were about to break off.

"There!" Peter cried.

The flashlight swung wildly and finally came to rest on a spot opposite them. The tops of the booths were just visible above the debris. Something long and shiny protruded from the water. At first, Carla thought it was a length of kelp, or maybe a stick, but it was moving, flicking upward like a long tongue. At the end of it was a triangular shape.

From behind her, Eric moved quickly down the stairs. The light from his camera bobbed across the water and then joined the pool of light from the flashlight. Carla could clearly see a tentacle, thick and smooth, a strange, silvery black color.

"It's still here," Peter said quietly. "Okay. Let's not do anything to agitate it. I want everyone to start moving back up the stairs, slowly and quietly, and that includes Eric. You hear me?"

"Yes."

"Should I turn the light off?" Eric whispered from behind her.

"No," Peter replied, voice low. "Just keep it steady. You too, Lucas."

To Carla's horror, the tentacle seemed to elongate. It began twisting around as if straining to hear. What if that's how it detected sound or motion? Through its stinger.

"Maybe we shouldn't…" The words dried up in Carla's throat.

Lucas gasped.

The tentacle froze.

Carla's heart turned to a block of ice in her chest. The triangular point lowered in their direction, and she heard Peter's swift intake of breath. Then, with a menacing flick, the long, smooth limb vanished into the murk, and the mass of debris parted in the middle.

The owner of the tentacle hurtled toward them.

Peter pointed his gun at the spot, but Yuki shoved past him and pushed Lucas against the wall with her hip. Again and again, she pulled the trigger of the gun, firing continuously at the creature now just a few feet away from her. In the tight space of the stairwell, the sound was thunderous, overpowering the continuous crash of the waves and Peter's frantic yelling.

Behind it, a second thing emerged from the water, the puckered mouth of its hideous human-like face seeming to snarl up at them. Yuki pulled the trigger again, but nothing happened. With a cry of frustration and fury, she hurled the gun at the creature. It bounced off its back and disappeared into the water.

It would have been comedic if Carla hadn't been so terrified. Her arms and her legs didn't seem to work. Lucas was pulling Yuki up the stairs, and suddenly, Peter was backing into Carla, the water erupting in front of them. They were down to one light now—the light from Eric's camera. There was no way of telling if the bullets from Yuki's gun had hit the thing, but at least it wasn't coming at them. It seemed to be thrashing around just below the surface.

Carla wondered why Peter wasn't firing at it, but her brain didn't seem to be sending the right signals to her throat, so the question went unasked.

Her ears registered the sounds of a struggle behind her. It was Yuki resisting Lucas's efforts to get her into the apartment. When Carla turned, it was just in time to see Yuki yank herself free and trip, hurtling past Eric and straight into her. The force of Yuki's body sent her crashing into Peter. Carla heard him grunt, then cry out, as he struggled not to lose his footing and fall into the water. When Carla turned, he was pulling himself into a standing position, both hands clutching the banister.

Both hands.

The second handgun was gone.

Chapter 22

winds gusting to 48 mph

Carla steered Peter toward the easy chair.

"That was a shitshow." Peter sighed loudly.

She grabbed a pillow from the couch and stuffed it behind his back, then kissed the top of his head. Her hands were trembling.

Yuki sat on the couch, staring down at her hands folded on her lap. "I'm sorry."

"Me too," Peter said grimly. "Because now we don't have any weapons, and we know those things are still down there."

"Thank God they can't climb the stairs." Carla stretched out at Peter's feet, one hand encircling his ankle. After the scare she just had watching Peter nearly fall into the water, she wanted the reassurance of his skin against hers. His ankle was clammy and cold. Or was that her hand?

"We'll just have to wait it out," Eric said. "Until the water goes down and help arrives."

Lucas pointed at the crack in the wall. "Aren't you forgetting something? We might not have a choice. We might have to leave." He turned to Peter. "Right? Shouldn't we be thinking of a Plan B?"

Peter shifted in his chair. "Probably." Leaning forward with a little groan and placing his elbows on his knees, he stared down at Carla. "The vacation rental is farther from the beach, so it might still be okay. If it is and if we can make it there and get down to the street, we should be able to get to the bandshell. The water's up to the steps, but if we can get there, we can climb up the bluff to San Refugio Heights. It's steep, and it'll be muddy, but we can do it."

Lucas eyed the floor. "That's a lot of 'ifs.'"

"We can hop over the balcony railing and get to Lucas's place, but the rental's balcony doesn't connect to it. We'll have to walk on another ledge, but it's a lot narrower than the one to Ken's apartment." Carla shrugged. "I can make it fine, but I'm not sure about everyone else."

"I can do it," Lucas said. "You and I can go check it out, see if it's in good shape."

Suddenly, Yuki was crying. "I'm so sorry. I shouldn't have done that. I've put everyone in danger. Matt would be so furious with me."

Eric looked up from his laptop. "You weren't lying when you said you knew how to shoot. It's just too bad you didn't kill it."

"Dude. You don't know that," Lucas snapped. "Maybe she did."

Eric pointed at the laptop. "I do know that because I was rolling, remember? Look."

Carla joined the others around the coffee table, stomach dropping. The camera had caught the semi-automatic flying through the air, Peter smashing into the wall, their frantic expressions as they fled up the stairs, and behind them, a tentacle whipping through the air, coming down and smacking a step just behind them. Then, moments later, the one with the strange bulbous head emerged above the bottom landing, its round eyes staring after them.

"Fuck those things," Lucas said. Sweat beaded on his forehead.

Eric straightened in his chair, rewound the video, then hit pause. "They're still alive. We didn't kill them, but we managed to piss them off. Because that's the way it looks, right? Pissed off?" His voice rose. "Since when do fish have facial expressions? Those aren't just markings." He tapped the screen. "Those are eyes. That's a mouth. That's not exactly a nose, more like two holes. We can't see most of its body, but this one isn't very long. Not like that other one we saw earlier. And how's it holding its head above water like that? It seems to have a bit of a neck. How's it breathing?"

"Fish have gills," Lucas said, as if that settled the matter.

Eric's chin jutted out. "Is that a fish? Or something else? Because I've never seen a fish take notice of people like that."

"Seals do," Peter said, frowning. "So do otters. What if it's more of a marine mammal?"

"With a slimy body and a tentacle?" Eric persisted.

Peter ran a hand over his face. "I don't see where all this is getting us. Are you trying to make a point here?"

"Maybe," Eric said, the confidence draining from his voice. "So, this is weird…because…" His voice drifted off.

Carla gazed at the video paused on the screen. The creature's two round eyes stared back at her with a malevolence that made her shudder. She looked away.

"Because what, Eric?"

Eric's eyebrows lifted. "Because I feel like it knows we're up here, and it's waiting for us."

Chapter 23

wave height 18.1 ft

Carla and Lucas peered over Lucas's balcony. The ledge to the vacation rental was a foot and a half wide. Hugging the wall, her right arm raised like she was taking a barre class, Carla inched her way across the span. It was longer and narrower than she remembered, at least three times the distance between her place and Ken's. Plus, the building took a sharp left turn before the balcony on the far side, and the ledge curved along with it.

The waves crashed into the building below, sending spray upward, mixing with the rain blowing sideways into her face and hampering her visibility. When Carla reached the curve, she felt herself wobble, heart hammering in her chest. She swiped the rain from her eyes before taking each step.

Whenever she paused, Lucas would shout, "I'm okay," behind her.

At least they could see. Sort of. Peter had secured flashlights to the upper sleeves of their jackets, using electrical tape to lash them in place. The light bounced every time she moved her left arm, but it was better than nothing, and they were finally getting closer to the sliding glass door and the warm yellow light glowing inside it.

And then she was climbing over the balcony railing. When Lucas was standing safely beside her, she peered through the glass.

A woman was pacing in the middle of the spacious room, one hand pressed against her mouth. She wore yellow pajama bottoms covered in a puppy pattern and a thin white tank top, knotless braids hanging down her back. The woman looked more like a college student than the well-dressed techie who'd visited her restaurant earlier that evening.

Carla knocked on the glass. The woman whirled around, eyes going wide, mouth shaping a scream. Then she ran toward them, fumbling with the lock.

"Oh, thank God," she said. "I was freaking out. Our phones don't work, and Olivia hasn't come back. She told me to stay here, but it's been forever and…"

The woman would have continued rambling if Carla hadn't stopped her. She re-introduced herself and Lucas and explained where they'd come from. "What's your name?"

"Natalie," she said, nervously eyeing the door across the room.

Carla's eyes took in the coffee table—two empty champagne bottles, a pastry box, an empty bag of ghost pepper potato chips, and lots of crumbs. They'd partied, and then the storm struck. Lucas shrugged out of his wet jacket and dropped it on the patch of tile in front of the glass door. Carla did the same.

"Where did Olivia go?" Carla said.

Natalie pressed a hand against her temple. "Downstairs. To see if maybe we could get out the front and go home." She gestured at the far wall. "There are no windows facing the street, so we couldn't see what's going on out there."

Carla thought for a moment. Both women were from Los Angeles and weren't familiar with San Refugio. They'd had too much to drink, which messed with their judgment. From what she remembered of their time at the restaurant, Olivia had been the more boisterous of the two. Carla could easily imagine Olivia saying, "I'll go look. It's no big deal," completely underestimating the danger.

"How long has she been gone?" Lucas said.

"An hour, maybe?" Natalie sounded uncertain.

Feigning a calm she didn't feel, Carla said, "Lucas, why don't you wait here with Natalie while I take a look downstairs."

Lucas scowled. "Um, that would be a 'no.'" A muscle in his jaw twitched. "Nothing is going to happen to Natalie up here. I'm coming with you."

Natalie was too distressed to catch the meaning behind his words. "I'll be fine."

Lucas licked his lips. "You wouldn't happen to have any guns, would you?"

"Me?" Natalie squeaked. "No! I'm, like, totally against guns. Why?"

Carla shot Lucas a look, grabbed him by the arm, and steered him toward the door before he could say anything else.

"What's going on? Why are you asking me about guns?" Natalie's voice had begun to waver, as if she might cry.

One hand on the doorknob, Carla made a big show of rolling her eyes. "This young man has watched too many action movies."

They'd almost reached the front door, when Lucas darted into the galley kitchen and began rummaging through the drawers. Natalie watched, perplexed. He took something out of the drawer, snatched two electric lanterns off the counter, and bounded across the room.

"Just getting a screwdriver in case the door's jammed," Lucas said over his shoulder, nudging Carla through the front door. When he closed it behind them, he held up a large chef's knife. "Just in case."

She had to give the young man credit. He was resourceful.

Lanterns in hand, they descended the staircase. Unlike the stairs leading to her apartment, these were well constructed, with even, wooden steps and a polished banister. The white-painted walls were decorated with colorful photographs of San Refugio Beach and Village. The stairwell turned, so it was impossible to see the bottom, but from the moisture in the air and the sound of churning water, she knew the ocean had found its way inside.

When they rounded the second landing, Carla bit her lip and surveyed the scene. The stairs ended in a vestibule, with one door to the street and two others in the wall under the stairs. Except for the side facing the street, the vestibule was made entirely of plate glass. It had filled with water and resembled one of the enclosures at the Monterey Bay Aquarium.

With the door closed, Carla couldn't understand how the water had come in, and then Lucas pointed at the floor. Like her restaurant, the waves had pushed up the floorboards. Splintered chunks of old, heavy wood bobbed around in the murky water. The bottom three steps were soaked.

"Where is Olivia, then?" Lucas asked.

The only way out was through the vestibule. Even in her drunken state, Carla couldn't imagine Olivia would have dared open the door.

She thought for a moment. "Maybe she made it out before the storm surge. Natalie said she'd been gone for about an hour, but she could be mistaken. Maybe it was longer."

The steps creaked behind her. Lucas shone his light toward the right of the vestibule.

"Where's that door go?"

"To the old kombucha place. It's vacant now. I think that other door goes to a real estate office. She could have gone into either one."

"Why would she do that?"

"She might have wanted to see what was going on out there." Carla pointed at the solid metal door leading to the street. "You can't see out from here."

Lucas cleared his throat. "So, what are we going to tell Natalie? I mean, she's already freaked out. If we tell her about…what we saw…"

"And she's still buzzed." Carla sighed.

Upstairs, Natalie leapt to her feet when they entered. Her shoulders sagged when she saw they were alone. "Oh my God, you didn't find her?"

Carla shook her head and shot Lucas a warning glance. "No, but we couldn't get outside, so it's possible she made it out before things got too bad and went to look for help. I'm sorry, but there's nothing we can do…"

"But she might be in trouble!" Natalie shouted, panic on her face.

Carla dipped her head. "She might. It's not the best idea to head outside during a storm like this."

Natalie let out a long breath, then sank back into the chair. It was covered in yellow velvet, the same color as her pajama bottoms. She chewed a nail.

"I told her not to go. I begged her. I mean, we were fine, watching movies on the computer and stuff. But Olivia said if we didn't leave, we might get stuck, and we both need to be at work on Monday. I mean, like, *have* to. A client is coming all the way from London, so she was beginning to panic. We were planning to drive back to L.A. on Saturday. We have an all-hands meeting on Sunday to prepare."

Carla could feel Lucas staring at her, willing her to tell Natalie the truth. They could, she supposed. Show her the video and the picture. But who knew how she'd take it, especially in her condition. Natalie had downed an entire bottle of champagne and was still slurring her words.

Carla looked around, scanning the walls for damage. None that she could see. Lucas took the hint and inspected the bedroom and bathroom. When he was done, he shook his head. Which meant the apartment was in better shape than hers.

"Maybe we should all move in here?" Lucas said.

He was right, of course. If only she thought Peter could make it across that ledge.

Chapter 24

sustained winds of 38 mph

Peter could tell something had changed. Carla and Lucas stood side-by-side, drenched, looking like co-conspirators.

"What happened?" he asked. Even to his own ears, he sounded suspicious.

Lucas wiped his face dry, then rubbed his wet hair. He turned to Carla expectantly.

Yuki handed Carla a towel, dark eyes questioning. The circles under Carla's eyes were more pronounced, and her lips were pinched.

"Well?" Peter prompted. The drugs he'd taken to ease the pain in his back were wearing off. He wished like hell he'd taken his doctor's advice and started physical therapy. Maybe he could have avoided unnecessary agony. It was a miracle his back hadn't given out on him completely, after everything he'd been through.

Carla remained standing, pressing the towel against her hair. "Well, one of the girls next door decided to see if she could get to their car…"

"In this storm?" Yuki's mouth puckered in disapproval.

Carla nodded. "In this storm. While shit faced." She draped the towel around the back of a chair.

Peter listened to the rest of the story. "How does it look over there? What kind of shape is the apartment in?"

Carla shrugged. "Better."

"How much better?" Peter pressed.

"No second-floor damage that we could see," Lucas replied.

Eric got to his feet. "Then what are we doing here? We should go." He turned to Peter. "It's closer to the bandshell, like you said. When the water level begins to drop, that part of the street will dry out first, and bam, we're out of here."

"Maybe." Carla shrugged. "If we can get there. Even for me, that was a tough walk on the ledge. It's even narrower than I thought, and there's some tricky spots. I'm seriously concerned that you could fall. Hell, I almost fell."

"Yeah, she did." Lucas nodded grimly. "Scared the fuck out of me."

Eric turned his palms to the ceiling. "What choice do we have? Peter said this place might collapse, and if it does, I prefer not to go down with it. We stand a better chance over there, right? It's worth the risk, right?"

"You might fall," Carla said stubbornly.

"I might die when the walls cave in here," Eric replied, bending to snatch up his backpack from the floor.

Yuki eyed the glass door and the darkness beyond. "How bad is the ledge?"

Carla hesitated. "I think you can do it."

Suddenly, Peter understood. "You don't think *I* can make it."

"Probably not," she said in a low voice. "I'd be afraid for you to try."

Peter's stomach clenched. Jesus. He couldn't remember feeling so emasculated, and the way Carla was trying not to make him appear weak in front of the others just added to his humiliation.

Eric's eyebrows shot up. "Wasn't he a big-time lifeguard or something, rescuing people? Are you saying he can't make it from here…to there?"

Yuki glared at Eric. "The job pretty much ruined his back. If Carla says it's not safe, then we should just stay here."

"That's not what she just said. She said it's not safe for him. *I'll* be fine. Lucas is fine. You'll be fine. Peter is welcome to stay here, and so is she."

Carla shook her head. "I think we need to stay together. Safety in numbers. We don't know what's going to happen next."

"Yeah, we do!" Eric barked out a laugh. "The building is going to collapse, and we'll land in the wave pool downstairs with Mr. Stinger and Ms. Face." He snapped shut the lid of his laptop and stuffed it into his backpack, then jerked his head at Lucas. "Are you coming with me? They can't tell you what to do, you know? Peter is not in charge, and neither is she."

Yuki's nostrils flared. "Hey, you little shit. This is Carla's place. She didn't invite you. You just showed up and made yourself at home. My husband said Peter saved so many lives since we moved here fifteen years ago that he lost count. Matt would say we need to do whatever Peter thinks we should do." She pointed at the sliding door. "If you want to leave, then leave. Get the hell out of here."

Peter stared at Yuki in surprise. He couldn't remember her ever being so angry. Maybe it was grief. Or maybe the guy had just pissed her off.

Peter held up a hand. "I think Carla's right. We should stick together, and Eric is right too. We're all better off next door. You guys go on ahead. I'll just take my time getting there." He stood and pushed his shoulders back, with more confidence than he felt.

When he glanced over at Carla, the color had left her face. He reached out and grasped her hand.

Chapter 25

wave height 16.7 ft

Eric went first. Even with his backpack, the reporter had no trouble navigating the narrow ledge connecting Lucas's apartment with the vacation rental next door. Yuki was next. Halfway across, she looked over her shoulder and smiled, as if to reassure him it wasn't so bad. Peter marveled at her balance and vowed to take up yoga. She'd been after him for years to try it. He'd probably be thinner, more flexible, and have better balance if he had.

Lucas followed.

If he lost his footing, Peter was planning to let himself fall into the water. If one of those things got him, so be it. He wasn't about to drag Lucas or Carla in with him.

Peter climbed over the balcony railing and stepped onto the narrow strip of stucco. The ledge was even smaller than he'd expected. Half of his body hung over the side, and he had to press against the wall to counteract the feeling he was about to topple into the waves. Back when he was still able to surf, he'd traversed narrower ledges than this one, some of them just inches wide, cut into the cliffs to help surfers get in or out of the water. He'd never had trouble with those. Surfing required a strong core and good balance. But when he stopped surfing, both had gone to hell, and he was paying for it now.

Despite the wind, the storm-chilled air, and the splash of the waves, he could feel sweat trickling down his back.

"I'm right behind you," Carla said.

Her bright, reassuring tone made him cringe. Not long ago, he was the one talking people through their fears.

Peter didn't reply. All his focus was on his size-twelve feet and the narrow strip of stucco. The temptation to turn his head toward the ocean, even just for a moment, was so powerful, his neck ached from locking his muscles into place.

He made slow progress and, in a few minutes, approached the vacation rental's balcony.

"There's that curve coming up," Carla warned.

Peter raised his right hand in acknowledgment. A mistake.

The slight movement disoriented him and made his left side peel away from the wall, forcing him to raise his right foot to counteract the imbalance. Carla cried out behind him. Lucas heaved himself on top of the balcony railing and leaned precariously over the side, arms outstretched.

As Peter struggled to regain his balance, Lucas grabbed his left arm and pulled him to the balcony. Peter flopped over the rail and landed on the deck.

His muscles felt like Jello. As he wiped his rain-splattered face, he noticed his hands were trembling. *Jesus.* He was so overcome with relief, he'd forgotten Carla, still behind him. Lucas hadn't. The young man helped her over the slick railing. Peter cursed his thoughtlessness.

The balcony was a tight squeeze for all three of them, so Lucas ducked inside.

Peter got to his feet. He was pulling Carla into a quick embrace when he saw something hurtling through the air toward them. Peter had just enough time to take a step through the doorway, bringing Carla along with him, before it crashed onto the balcony with a sickening thud, nearly hitting them both.

From behind him, he heard shouting, but it hardly registered. Peter stared down at a woman's body lying motionless at his feet. Her head was twisted at an impossible angle. Her clothes were tattered. Horrible gashes covered her face, and terror was etched into its once beautiful features.

Carla let out an anguished cry and recoiled.

The dead woman had red hair, but some of it was missing, revealing the pale, bloodied scalp below. Peter kneeled over her, fear coursing through his veins.

"Oh my God, Olivia," Natalie was shouting.

Olivia. That was her name. This woman who flew through the air as if someone had placed her body in a catapult and launched it. At them.

The rain continued to pour down around them.

Peter peered over the railing cautiously, in case something else came flying at him. An object seemed to be moving in the angry water. Lucas joined him in the rain, shining the beam of his flashlight into the murky darkness.

An improbable face bobbed just above the surface, its body hidden by the waves, and far behind it, a muscular tentacle rose into the air.

"Fuckity fuck fuck," Lucas said in a stage whisper.

That thing, the creature with the knowing, staring eyes, had flung Olivia's body onto the balcony, like a fish tossed onto the deck of a boat.

Chapter 26

winds gusting to 36 mph

Just a few hours ago, Peter had sat in Carla's restaurant, shooting the shit with Quint and Ken, and now Ken was in a coma, Matt was dead, and a body had literally been dropped at his feet. He felt numb, but there was a fire smoldering deep inside of him, an unwillingness to give in to pain, a determination to survive the storm and whatever it had brought ashore.

Yuki and Lucas stayed inside with Natalie. She'd screamed herself hoarse after seeing her friend's mangled corpse and was now sobbing, clinging to Lucas. Yuki retreated to the couch, staring off into space, hands clenched into fists.

Eric had insisted on recording the inspection of the woman's body on the balcony, the storm pelting them with rain. He hovered over Peter, who knelt next to Olivia. Carla crouched beside him, a flashlight in her unsteady hand.

The light from Eric's camera added to the unreality of the moment.

As Eric continued to film, Peter examined Olivia's body, noting every detail.

Unlike Maggie, her eyes were still intact. Her clothes were ripped, her skin scraped. The creature with the face had a tentacle and a stinger, but so far, he saw no sign of a stab wound.

Carla seemed to read his mind. "Let's turn her over."

Olivia had been tall and thin. Peter guessed she couldn't weigh more than 130 pounds. It seemed wrong to shift her.

The back of the woman's head revealed more chunks of missing hair. The white skin on her scalp was ragged and torn. Deep gouges ran along her neck, and there, just to the right of where the cervical met the thoracic spine, was a hole ringed in black slime. Peter's stomach lurched at the sight.

He'd seen death before. Drownings, mostly. Falls from cliffs. A few shark attacks. But this was something else entirely. The wound was as sinister as the monster that had inflicted it.

"Same as Matt." Carla didn't sound surprised.

"Can you move a little so I can get a better shot," Eric said. "You're in my way."

Peter sighed. The guy was just doing his job, and they were experiencing the story of the century. If they lived long enough to tell it. He couldn't order the reporter to stop filming.

"Let's get out of the rain." Peter pushed himself to his feet. The effort made his back spasm, and he cursed, more from irritation than pain.

When they were inside, the sliding door locked behind them. Peter pulled Carla into the bathroom and kicked the door shut.

The marble counter was covered with tubes and pots of makeup. Carla snatched a towel from a ring and rubbed his wet hair, her dark eyes staring into his.

"Why did it do that?" she asked. "Throw her body at us like that?"

Peter shook his head. "I don't know. It's not behaving like any animal I've ever seen. Maybe it's the one Ken captured and put in that tank. Maybe it remembers and figures humans are dangerous, and we're the only humans around. So, it killed Olivia, and it wanted us to know about it? But I'm just guessing."

Carla flung the towel into the tub and grabbed another from a rack above the toilet. She patted her face. "All those marks on her. It wasn't trying to eat her, was it? That's not how it looks to me."

Peter shook his head. "I don't think so. I've seen shark bites before. This looks nothing like those."

Carla leaned against the sink, arms folded across her chest. Her hair had come undone, and it made her look vulnerable. "What are we going to do?"

"Avoid them, for one. We're safe here." He paused. "I think."

Carla covered her face with her hands and groaned. "I can't believe this is happening. How much longer is this high tide going to last? And then what?"

"We stay here until the tide goes out and help arrives."

"But what about those things?"

"Hopefully, they'll go out with the tide." Peter pulled Carla to him. She was shaking.

"What if they don't?"

"Whatever they are, they probably have gills, so they need to be in water. We've never seen them on the beach before, have we? The storm brought them in, and it will probably take them out." Peter gestured toward the window. "No one really knows what's out there in the deep. Hopefully, they'll go back to where they came from."

"Maybe." Carla's voice was faint, uncertain. "I'm so tired. I wish we could sleep. Damn Ken. This is all his fault."

"We don't know that."

Carla pulled away, crossed her arms in front of her chest, and stared up at him. "Pretty sure we do. He caught one, and the next thing we know, Matt's dead. What if those things can communicate with each other? What if the one Ken trapped was sending out messages for help to its freaky friends and that's why that other one showed up in my restaurant? Think about it, Peter. We don't know how many are out there."

A wave of cold passed through him. Carla could be right, but even if she was, there wasn't much they could do about it. She rested her head against his chest. He wrapped his arms around her and held her until he felt her body relax against his own.

The tide would go out. All they needed to do—all they *could* do—was wait.

Chapter 27

wave height 15.6 ft

Carla wished she could stay locked in the bathroom with Peter, the two of them stretched out in the nice big spa tub with a pile of fluffy oversized bath towels, door locked until the sun came up.

But that was not happening. And in a way, their ordeal was just beginning. Assuming they escaped in one piece, people would need to be told about the creatures. The consequences would be enormous. Who in their right mind would want to come to San Refugio with those things around? People and businesses around the Monterey Bay would be hit hard. And maybe not just the bay. Maybe south to San Diego and north up to San Francisco and Sonoma County.

What if this was just the beginning? What if more of those things were out there?

It was too much.

But honestly, as nasty as they were, they were just another predator. The world had plenty of those, and people had learned how to deal with them.

As soon as they reentered the living room, Natalie leapt to her feet. "What the hell killed my friend?" She jerked her head in the direction of Yuki and Lucas. "I'm not getting much out of them."

Yuki sat in a chair as if frozen, but when Carla drew closer, she saw her friend was crying silently, tears streaming down her face.

Lucas appeared sapped of life, sitting on the floor, slumped against the sofa. The only one with any energy was Eric. Braving the deluge, he'd gone back out on the balcony with his camera.

Natalie deserved an answer. Carla just hoped she'd be able to process it after all the champagne she'd had earlier in the evening.

"We don't know exactly. You heard about the two men who were killed by something venomous in the water?" When Natalie nodded, she continued. "We thought it was something like a stingray, but we've seen them, and that's not what they are. They're bigger. And smarter. And they're in my flooded restaurant…and outside too."

"We think the storm brought them in," Peter added, collapsing into the closest chair.

Natalie tipped back her head, hands balled into fists. "But…what are they? That's not normal for fish. It's not…normal!" She glared at Peter, lips trembling. "You're supposed to be the beach expert or something. Can you explain this?"

Peter shook his head sadly. "I cannot. I'm sorry. I'm just as mystified as everyone else. All I know is, they're dangerous, and we need to do everything we can to avoid them."

Natalie's mouth fell open. She threw her hands up in the air. "That's it? That's all I get? My friend was killed by something in the water, and it threw her body at us, and that's all you can say? I don't know? It's something dangerous? Wow. Really? Wow."

Lucas's head slowly swiveled toward Natalie. "Whoa. I know you're freaking out, but can you not be such a bitch about it?"

Natalie's eyes flashed with anger. "Excuse me? I'm a bitch because I want answers? Because I want to know what killed my friend?"

Carla shot Lucas a warning glance before turning back to Natalie. "Look, we're all scared here, but we're just being honest. We're cut off by the storm, and we're not scientists. We can't just snap our fingers and come up with answers that will make you happy. But you're right about one thing. They're not normal fish."

Natalie nodded and sank into the chair next to Peter. "Sorry," she said, voice softening. "I just can't believe this is happening. I mean, me and Olivia came here for a fun weekend, and now she's dead. And there's monster fish out there, and the building is falling apart."

Carla watched Natalie cover her face with her hands. Lucas rolled his eyes and stared up at the ceiling. With nothing else to say, Carla went into the kitchen. The young women had managed to make a mess in the short time they'd been in the place. Carla found a tin of fancy dark hot chocolate in a cupboard and, miracle of miracles, a carton of fresh milk. She made it the old-fashioned way, on the gas stove, then topped each mug with a sprinkle of cinnamon.

Lucas wrapped both hands around the mug like a child and sipped. "Thanks, Mom," he said, then smiled sheepishly.

Carla was so shocked to hear that word on his lips, her hands spasmed and hot chocolate spilled all over the coffee table. She rushed into the kitchen to grab some napkins so no one could see the tears in her eyes. It wasn't Lucas's fault he reminded her of her son, she reminded herself sternly. She was a grownup, and she should start acting like one, quit behaving like a cranky old bitch. Counting to twenty and taking deep breaths made it possible for her to return with a fresh mug of hot chocolate and a dish towel to mop up the mess.

Peter was studying her, eyebrows knitted together. He was about to say something when the sliding door opened, letting in a blast of chilly air.

"It's out there," Eric announced. "Like it's waiting for something."

They all turned to stare at him.

Lucas's dark eyes went wide over the top of the mug. "What the actual fuck?"

Eric set his camera down on the bistro table in front of the windows and carefully removed the plastic hood beaded with rain drops. "The actual fuck is worse than you think." His voice was steely. "Has anyone bothered to take a close look at Olivia?"

Natalie stared at the reporter in horror, a hand pressed to her mouth.

Peter lurched to his feet. "What's that supposed to mean?"

Eric gestured behind him. "I mean, something's happening to her, and it's not good."

Dread was a cold hard hand pressing against Carla's back, forcing her to follow Peter outside. Lucas was on her heels, holding an electric lantern.

Silently, they stared down at the pale dead woman. Silvery black streaks stretched from the hole in her back, disappearing under her tattered sweatshirt. They snaked across the bits of scalp between the horrible gaps in her hair. The skin on either side of the streaks had taken on a sinister sheen, giving the impression of a shadow slowly spreading.

Before anyone could stop him, Eric used the tip of his boot to nudge the body over. Electric tingles raced up the

144

back of Carla's legs. Gasping, she clutched Peter's arm. Olivia's face was now a mottled gray. Her mouth appeared puckered and sunken, the edges around her lips black. A streak ran between the side of her mouth to an ear. Black fluid oozed out and down her neck.

Lucas was first to break the stunned silence. "What's happening to her?"

"It's probably the venom," Peter said.

Carla thought back to earlier in the day. It seemed so long ago now. "Remember what Quint said about the guy who got stung, who ended up in the hospital? He turned purple."

"I'm worried about what happens next," Eric said.

Lucas gave a nervous cough. "What do you mean?"

The lantern swayed. Everyone's eyes were wide and frightened. Natalie, huddled in the doorway, was breathing raggedly.

Eric gripped the back of a chair. "I can't believe I have to spell this out for you. What if those things are like vampires…or zombies? But they sting instead of biting, and their venom is like a virus that infects the person. And then they're transformed into…whatever those things are."

"Jesus," Peter muttered. "That's a little out there, don't you think?"

"No!" Eric exploded. "It's not. There are things in the water with tentacles and human faces. We don't know what they are or what they're capable of. And look at her! She's getting worse as we stand around, trying to decide what to do."

Peter scowled. "What are you suggesting?"

"Are you saying we should tie her up or something?" Carla asked, voice rising. They'd already treated the dead woman with such disrespect, leaving her out on the balcony instead of bringing her inside and covering her with a sheet.

Eric rubbed the side of his face. He shot an uneasy glance at Natalie and in a low voice said, "We need to get rid of it. Throw it over the side. We can't risk it being up here with us."

Carla tensed, her hands balling into fists. "Eric, that's a woman you're talking about. Someone's best friend. Someone's child. Her. You mean *her*."

Eric mouth stretched into a straight stubborn line. "Not anymore, and who knows what she's going to be when the venom is finished with her. We can't leave her up here. It's not safe." He looked around expectantly. "Who's going to help?"

Carla gazed at Olivia's body, suddenly uncertain. Was it her imagination, or were the streaks on her face becoming darker? While she hesitated, Lucas disappeared inside.

A few moments later, he returned with two pairs of yellow rubber gloves. "I found these under the sink."

Carla watched in growing disbelief as the two young men pulled them on, expressions grim. She bit back a curse and turned to Peter instead. "Are you okay with this?"

"I'm not, but what if he's right?" Peter said with a bitter edge.

Behind them, Natalie wailed. "I can't believe this is happening!"

Yuki sidled up to Carla and took her arm. "Do you think that happened to Matt too?" Her voice was flat.

If so, it happened out of sight at the hospital, most likely after an orderly had slid his body into a mortuary cabinet. If Matt had turned into one of those things, at least he'd be in there. Did they lock them? Carla had no idea, but she couldn't stop thinking about the horror of it. Would reanimated Matt need sea water to survive? She shook her head to banish the ridiculous, unwanted image of zombie Matt trying to claw his way out of cold storage.

Yuki hadn't expected an answer. She was watching Lucas and Eric maneuver Olivia's corpse toward the railing. Carla stared, bile rising in the back of her throat, as the woman's red hair trailed over the bright yellow of Lucas's glove.

They heaved the body over the side of the railing. Carla had one last glimpse of a pale ankle, silvery black streaks crawling upward from the underside of her delicate foot.

And then, a splash.

And in that moment, Carla imagined her son thrown out of a boat in the middle of the Monterey Bay, arms pinwheeling. She choked back the sob rising in her throat.

Chapter 28

tide 4.3 ft

Yuki went straight into the kitchen, returned with a tall glass of water, and held it out to Natalie. "You need to rehydrate after all that wine. Drink this," she commanded. "All of it."

Lucas sat at the bistro table, quiet and miserable, body angled away.

Eric leaned forward. "Natalie, this is probably a bad time to ask, but I was wondering, when everything has settled down, if you wouldn't mind giving me an interview about your friend?"

Natalie's head slowly swiveled toward him. Her mouth opened, then closed. She stared at Eric for a long time before a cold hard smile came to her face, replacing the lost, dazed expression. "Of course. After you tell your audience about how you chucked my best friend into the ocean like catch-and-release. Then you can ask whatever you want. What the fuck is wrong with you? Who even watches TV news anymore?"

Lucas smirked. "Oh snap."

Natalie shot Eric her middle finger.

Eric sat back, stung—for once, speechless.

Nerves already frazzled, Carla's temper flared. She rapped her knuckles against the table. "Do not make me come over there." As soon as the words were out of her mouth, she knew what was coming next and steeled herself.

"Okay, Mom," the young men replied in unison.

There was nothing else to do but go along with it. She shot them her best mom-stare, and to her surprise and relief, it broke the tension.

A crash came from the direction of the front door.

Carla felt the floor vibrate beneath her feet, followed by a noise like a giant was kicking the walls over and over. Natalie cried out in alarm. A large canvas print of a whale breeching in the bay fell off the wall. A white vase with white winter roses toppled off a shelf and shattered on the wooden floor.

Then everything was quiet.

Carla's heart raced. She needed to get up and investigate, but her limbs were paralyzed with dread.

Lucas raised a hand in the air, as if testing the temperature. "Was that an earthquake?"

The noise started up again, an ominous creaking and splintering of wood.

Eric was looking around frantically. "That doesn't sound good."

"We gotta figure out what's going on. This place could be coming down." Carla found herself moving toward the front door, Peter on her heels.

"Don't!" Natalie bellowed. "You don't know what's out there."

Carla paused. The noise outside the door started up again. From the bedroom, something fell off a wall. Glass shattered.

She was reaching for the handle when Natalie screamed. "Stop! What if it's Olivia? What if she's come back?"

Carla's hand froze. Dear God. Come back as what? Nothing they'd seen was big enough to cause the pounding making the floors vibrate.

She felt two hands come down on her shoulders and gently but firmly move her aside. Peter opened the door, revealing the nightmare beyond.

Chapter 29

49°

The stairs outside the door were gone. The entire staircase had detached from the wall, a crooked and twisted thing supported—barely—by the landing below. It was like looking into a funhouse mirror distorting whatever you were looking at, but Peter did not doubt his eyes. The stairs were several feet from the door with a wide gap separating them from the walls on either side, which were tilted at odd angles.

"The foundation must be in worst shape than I thought." Carla came up beside him.

Peter clutched the doorway for support. At least *that* was still standing. "This shouldn't be happening. This is practically brand-new construction."

When he glanced down at Carla, the whites of her eyes seemed to glow. "It's not. Not really. They moved some walls around, but the structure is still original, just with a new facade and fresh paint."

Peter groaned. They'd moved to the vacation rental, thinking it was safer than the other buildings, but the entire row was built on pilings, making it vulnerable to the raging sea.

And whatever was swimming in it.

Peter stepped back and closed the door. "We have to get out of here."

"And go where?" Carla turned her palms upward.

"Back to your place. Or even Ken's."

Carla eyed him nervously. "Will you be able to make it back okay? On the ledge?"

"Sure," he said gruffly. "I'll have to. Staying here is not an option, and we need to do something quickly, in case the whole place comes down."

Carla rubbed the side of her face. "Peter, I know we don't need more bad news, but before we found you in the men's room, when we were down in the kitchen bringing up food, I thought I smelled gas. Lucas and Eric didn't notice anything, so maybe it's nothing."

"With the beating the building has taken, it wouldn't surprise me if some pipes have come loose." Peter shrugged, unconcerned, his tone distracted as he thought of the return journey across the ledge.

The group gathered behind him.

Eric had the camera out again, recording. Eye pressed to the viewfinder, he said, "Peter, can you please explain what you're seeing out there? And then I'll grab some quick shots."

"You can't help yourself, can you?" Natalie snarled.

"Nope," Lucas said. "He can't."

Peter was in no mood to give interviews. "I'm not an official anymore, remember?" he growled, pushing past the reporter, Carla's hand firmly in his own. "All right, everyone. This building isn't as stable as we hoped it would be. In fact, it's probably worse than the others. We need to get out of here. Back to Carla's, or maybe even Ken's place. It's the farthest building that we can actually get to, and we need as much distance as possible between us and this place if it collapses."

As if to emphasize the point, a thundering crash came from the stairwell.

Natalie reacted with surprising speed. She darted into the bedroom and emerged holding an orange backpack. "You don't have to tell me twice," she said, shoving her feet into sneakers.

Peter scowled when he noticed her choice of footwear. "Do you have anything with a firmer sole? The ledge over to Lucas's place is narrow."

Natalie ran back to the bedroom and came out, clutching a pair of Doc Martens. Peter studied them, wondering why a young woman would choose a pair of shoes that looked like they belonged to Frankenstein, but with those treads, she'd be fine.

When they had their jackets on and hoods up, he stepped outside onto the balcony, holding up a warning hand for everyone to stay back. The rain and wind were much lighter.

He shone his lantern down and swept the light over the water. Just waves. No corpse bobbing around. No sea creature gazing up at him with a menacing stare.

"I'll go first, if Lucas holds the light for me," Yuki said.

Before Peter could reply, Yuki was over the balcony railing, and Lucas was pushing past him to follow.

Natalie stepped out onto the balcony, took one look at the ledge, and gasped. "Are you fucking kidding me?"

"That would be a no," Eric snapped. "And don't worry. I don't have my camera out, so if you fall, I won't be capturing the moment."

Natalie marched in place, shaking her head. "I'm not sure I can do this."

"You'll be fine," Carla said sternly. "Because the alternative is staying here while the walls come down around you. You go ahead of me, and I'll talk you through it."

Peter took another deep breath. They had to go, but leaving was no guarantee of safety. It was possible the weight of the collapsing vacation rental would drag down the rest of the buildings in the row. When they made it across—*if* they made it across—he'd have to ask Carla if there was any way to get to Amalia's place at the very end.

Natalie gazed up at him with terrified eyes, as if beseeching him to do something. To save her. He understood. Peter was no happier about stepping out onto the ledge than she was.

"We'll be right behind you," he said.

She raised one leg over the balcony railing and gave a little cry. "This totally sucks."

He watched, feeling helpless, as she mashed herself against the wall, the breeze lifting her locs. She took one step, and he realized her mistake. The backpack was throwing off her balance. Natalie seemed to reach the same conclusion because her fingers released it, and it dropped into the darkness.

"I guess that means another trip to the DMV," she cried.

Bravado or nervous energy—whatever it took to get her across safely. She'd just lost her friend. Yuki had just lost her husband. That they both continued to function, to survive, took grit.

"You're doing great," he called after her.

"Liar," she shouted.

Peter watched her progress, his heart a hard lump in his throat. *Please don't let her fall. Please don't let her fall.*

Carla was bouncing on one foot, knuckles curled against her mouth. "Go next. Please."

"No." He shook his head. If he was going down, he wanted space between himself and Carla. He couldn't bring himself to admit he was feeling even more lightheaded than the last time he walked the ledge. His feet and legs tingled. Saliva pooled in his mouth, forcing him to swallow repeatedly. At this rate, he'd be peeing his pants next.

Lucas had reached his balcony and was helping Natalie over the railing. When both feet touched the concrete, she pumped a fist into the air. "Yes!"

Yuki hugged her. Eric was filming, but Natalie was too relieved to protest.

Lucas aimed his flashlight at the ledge. It swung up to Carla's knees, then to her face. "Okay, Carla. You've got this."

Peter could easily imagine her expression. The tilt of her head and set of her shoulders radiated exasperation. Carla didn't like condescension any more than he did.

"It would help if you didn't blind me," she shouted.

When the beam returned to the ledge, Carla swung herself over the balcony and hurried across as if something were chasing her.

There was nothing for Peter to do but follow.

The sliding door was open. Another thunderous crack boomed from the stairwell, reminding him there wasn't any time to waste. The extra weight he'd put on around his middle made him less flexible, and when he'd made it over the balcony rail, his left hip and thigh muscles ached with the effort. If it weren't for the tread on his shoes, he was sure he'd slip into the churning water below.

Just one more time. Just one more time.

Peter went slowly, positioning his foot on the ledge, checking its placement and grip before moving the next, ignoring the impatience radiating from Carla bouncing up and down on her toes. Her anxious gaze bore into him. His neck and shoulders ached with the fierce concentration the journey required. Around the curve and across the narrow strip of stucco.

If you make it, you've earned a whiskey shot.

The light from Eric's camera swung away from him and toward the water. Peter's head followed the light, which was now trained on the waves. Gritting his teeth, he forced his eyes back on the ledge where they belonged.

Carla was yelling, and so were Lucas and Eric. Peter froze. His feet felt like they were encased in concrete blocks. Were they telling him to hurry up or go back? And why? If he looked down at the water, he might lose his balance.

No. That's not what they were saying.

"Watch out!" Natalie screamed.

Those two words had to be the most unhelpful in the English language. Watch out for what? Where? How? In his circumstances, standing precariously on a ledge, he stiffened, bracing for whatever he was supposed to watch out for.

Now Carla was shrieking. Ice flooded his veins.

Something slammed into the wall, missing him by inches. He saw a flash of long red hair embedded with twigs and a puckered mouth filled with black slime.

Olivia. Again. What the hell?

With athleticism he thought had long ago left his body, Peter moved quickly across the remaining distance and hurled himself over the balcony railing before the creature below could relaunch its corpse missile and take him out. He fell on hands and knees, slamming into the concrete floor of the balcony with such force, his entire body juddered.

Hands helped him inside. The door slammed shut behind him.

Peter crawled across the tan tiles, batting away helping hands. When he reached a brown couch, he pushed himself to his feet. His lower back spasmed, and he toppled onto the lumpy sofa with a groan. An almost giddy relief bubbled up inside him, and he began to laugh. He'd survived the ledge and a flying corpse.

His back had gone out, but he was alive.

Chapter 30

storm surge 5.2 ft

Natalie was a babbling, crying mess. Carla asked Yuki to take her into Lucas's bedroom. Peter needed her attention now. The couch was too soft, so with Lucas's and Eric's help, they assisted Peter in moving to the floor, where he lay on his back, staring up at them and breathing raggedly.

"It almost got you," Lucas said.

Eric began pacing on the other side of the coffee table. "Yeah, almost. And you know what I think? I think it was waiting for just the right moment to try and take one of us out and maybe decided you were its best shot because you were the slowest. If I'm right, that means it's intelligent and capable of making decisions."

Carla stared at him for a long time.

Peter's arm was flung over his eyes. "That sounds about right to me."

Lucas cleared his throat. When Carla glanced over at him, he jerked his head at the wall behind the couch. The sheetrock was cracked and split. The place was crumbling around them, and the obvious escape routes were blocked by those damn things below. Carla felt like screaming.

"We can't stay here." She patted Peter's arm. "Do you think you can move? We need to get to Ken's place."

Peter moved his arm away. His face was white with pain. "I don't know. Maybe."

"Do you still have those pain pills?"

She bit her lip, watching him pat the front pocket of his sodden jeans. "Yes, but if I take them, I'll be out of it. Worse than useless."

Lucas raised his hand in the air, like a pupil asking a teacher for permission to speak. "I have something that might help."

Carla frowned. "Like what?"

Eric snorted. "I bet you do."

"Hey, back off dude," Lucas snapped. "I'd like to remind everyone that marijuana is legal in California, and I'm over the age of twenty-one. My grandpa has trouble with his back, so he gives me money to buy him something from a place in Santa Cruz. It's weed that's really good for pain. I was going to take it to him in Salinas this weekend, so I have it if you want to try it."

"That might be better than the pain pills," Carla said, smoothing the damp hair away from Peter's eyes. Over the summer, she and Peter had visited a dispensary that opened in San Refugio and were blown away by the soaring ceilings, modern furniture, and fancy display cases. The marijuana had blown them away too. It was not the pot they remembered from their youth. A few puffs had wiped them out.

Carla looked up at Lucas. "Will he still be able to function?"

Lucas shrugged. "I think so. He's younger and bigger than my grandpa. So maybe try a puff or two and see how it goes?" He crossed the room to the desk, opened a drawer, and held out a paper bag.

Carla gave Peter's arm a gentle squeeze. "Want to try it?"

He sighed. "I don't see that I have much choice if I want off the floor. It's worth a try."

Lucas opened a plastic pouch and handed a joint to Peter.

Eric continued pacing. "This is all great, and I hope your back feels better after you smoke that, but that doesn't solve our problem. We still need to get next door, and that means going outside. I don't know about you, but playing dodgeball with a corpse isn't my idea of a good time."

Carla waved a hand in front of her nose. The room suddenly reeked of pot. Peter inhaled, then began coughing. She went into the galley kitchen, poured him a glass of water, and held it to his lips while he sipped.

"I know it happened fast, but did you get a look at her, Peter? Did Olivia look…different?"

"No, I didn't get a good look. Not enough to see what was really going on with her," he said with a bitter edge. "But it doesn't matter. It's trying to kill us, or taunt us, or both, and going outside puts us at risk. It's got plenty of ammunition too. Sticks, logs, beach umbrellas…"

Carla couldn't believe this was happening. Any of it. They should be at a motel, safely sleeping through the storm, instead of running around, like rats trying to escape a sinking ship. She silently cursed the city manager for going with the wrong weather forecast.

"We could take turns keeping watch," Lucas reasoned. "We don't have a ledge to worry about anymore. It's just climbing from one balcony to the next. It's not like we'll fall into the water."

Peter took another small, cautious puff. "That thing has decent aim. You don't want to get hit with whatever it's throwing. And it's done it twice, so we can be pretty sure it'll try again."

"This is so messed up." Eric threw his head back and groaned.

Carla swiveled around to stare at the opposite wall. Her bedroom was on the other side, the wall thin enough that she could hear Lucas playing his video games. She turned to Lucas, who was crouched next to Peter, watching him intently.

"Lucas," Carla said, "do you have a hammer?"

Chapter 31

tide 3.9 ft

Carla sat on the floor next to Peter, holding his hand and watching Lucas widen the hole into her apartment. It took a few tries to find the right spot between the studs, but the hammer punched through the drywall easily enough. The dust released into the air made them sneeze and cough. The noise brought Yuki and Natalie into the living room, eyes wide. Carla quickly explained.

Natalie nodded. "That's a good idea." She shuddered. "I really don't want to go outside again."

Lucas wiped his face with the back of his sleeve and stepped aside, grinning, his teeth glowing white in the light of Eric's video camera. Eric wouldn't put the thing down, and everyone was too tired to protest.

Through the ragged opening, Carla could see her dresser against the wall of textured wallpaper Yuki had helped put up.

It was time to go, but first, they had to get Peter off the floor.

Carla stood over him. His head was turned toward the wall as he contemplated the hole.

"How you doing down there?"

"Better," he said cautiously. "I think." His eyes were bloodshot.

"Can you get up, or do you need some more time?"

Eric sniffed loudly. "That's one thing we *don't* have."

Natalie jammed her hands under her armpits. "You're freaking me out." Her voice was shrill.

Eric let out a loud breath but didn't reply.

Carla ignored them and focused on Peter. "Do you need help getting up?"

Peter grunted and rolled onto his side, then brought his knees to his chest with a groan. He grimaced and slowly maneuvered onto his hands and knees.

Lucas rushed over and placed a chair in front of Peter, then gripped the back. "Use the chair to push yourself up. That's how my grandpa does it."

Peter barked out a laugh, harsh and bitter. The mention of Lucas's grandfather seemed to give him the push he needed. The next moment, he was standing.

Yuki crossed the room and inspected the opening in the wall with a frown. "This will need to be bigger if Peter's going to get through it without bending over and throwing his back out again."

Lucas grabbed the hammer and set to work, widening the hole until it nearly reached the floor.

After some discussion of where to poke the next hole, Lucas began busting through the wall from Carla's living room into Ken's office, revealing the back of an enormous dark wood desk. It was too heavy to move but easy enough to climb over.

Natalie was the first to go through. Peter was next. The medical marijuana seemed to be working. When he'd made it over the desk, he lowered himself into Ken's easy chair and began to giggle helplessly.

"Oh, great. He's high." Natalie rolled her eyes, walked into the living room, and began screaming.

Eric nearly dropped his camera. Lucas raised the hammer above his head and charged into the living room. Carla glanced around wildly, looking for anything that could be used as a weapon, and snatched a pair of scissors from the desk.

Natalie was pressed against a wall, shaking uncontrollably. "There's a dead man in here!"

Carla let out a sigh and lowered her head. Ken.

"Natalie, I'm sorry, I should have warned you. Ken was in bad shape when Peter and I were over here. We didn't think he'd make it, and I should have thought about that before we broke through the wall."

Yuki hurried in, holding a blanket, which she gently draped over the still body of Ken Bigg.

Natalie sagged with relief. "Oh my God, I thought one of those things got in here and killed him."

"Nothing like that," Carla reassured her. "He was just in very poor health, and all this was too much for him."

Lucas set the hammer on the kitchen counter. "So now that we're here, what do we do?"

Peter walked into the living room, apparently recovered from his laughing fit. "We wait. The storm should be over soon."

"And hope the entire building doesn't collapse in the meantime," Eric said. He set his camera down on the coffee table and flopped into a leather recliner. "Oh man, this is a nice chair." He patted the arm rest. "I always thought these were, like, old people chairs, but now I want one." His head flopped back, and he closed his eyes.

Ken was now a large, lumpy presence on the couch, covered in a red, white, and blue bedspread decorated with anchors and sail boats. He was too big to move to the bedroom, so he'd have to stay where he was.

Carla asked Lucas and Eric to help her turn the couch so Ken faced the wall away from them.

Natalie and Yuki went into the hallway, returned with a pile of blankets, and handed them around.

"I don't think any of us can sleep," Yuki said, "but we can try to close our eyes."

Carla stared out a window at the darkness. A light rain pelted the glass. She pulled out her phone. Still no signal. The time read 5:14 a.m. More than an hour until dawn.

Chapter 32

storm surge 1.1 ft

Peter sat in a straight-back chair, afraid to get too comfortable. Somehow, he'd managed to doze off, and when his eyes flickered open, his heart lifted. The wall of darkness outside the windows was now gray, and the rain had tapered to a steady drizzle.

Carla stood by the window. Her hair had come loose, and she'd not bothered to tie it back. When she turned to him, the dark smudges under her eyes matched the color of the sky. In the recliner, Eric snored. The aroma of freshly brewed coffee filled the room. Lucas and Yuki were in the kitchen, pouring boiling water into a coffee filter. From the bathroom in the hallway, a toilet flushed.

Peter pushed himself to a standing position. The pot hadn't completely worn off. It seemed to have done some good. His back ached but in a vague sort of way, and he was mobile.

He joined Carla standing sentry at the window. "Anything out there?"

Her gaze flitted back to the view. "No. I haven't gone outside, but the tide seems to have gone out." She pointed at the deck below. The tables and chairs chained to Harmon's deck railings were now visible, toppled and draped in seaweed. "If the water level is that low back here, that means the street must be nearly dry. So, if we can make it to the door, we can get out of here. I'm worried about the building. It's been creaking and groaning."

Peter glanced down at her in alarm. "Has it?"

She nodded. "Yeah."

He rubbed a hand over his face, now covered in stubble. "I must have really passed out. I didn't hear a thing."

Carla squeezed his arm. "You weren't out for a long. Just about an hour or so."

He sighed. "Well, we'll have to go take a look."

They joined the others in the kitchen and drank coffee, too numb and weary to talk until the caffeine kicked in. When Peter announced their plan to go downstairs, Natalie's eyes snapped open.

"Is that such a good idea?" Now that she was sober, her demeanor had changed. Still nervous but more in control.

"Probably not," Peter admitted. "But who knows what's going on with this building? And if we need to leave in a hurry, I'd rather know what's going on down there first."

"We'll have to go through my place to do it," Carla added. "The staircase here leads to the back, which"—she glanced at Natalie—"we want to avoid."

"I hope it's more successful than our last expedition," Eric said, darting a glance at Yuki, who stiffened and stared into her mug.

Natalie studied him for a moment, eyebrows lifting. "Care to enlighten me?"

Eric shrugged. "Back at Carla's restaurant. It was a shitshow. Yuki thought she was John Wick and…" His voice trailed off.

The floor juddered.

Natalie grabbed the edge of the table. "Did you feel that?"

The group froze, looking at each other with wide eyes. Another tremor shook the floor, more violent this time.

Dread squeezed Peter's chest—a now familiar and disturbing feeling. Adrenaline spiked in his veins, and he shot to his feet. "We need to go."

They rushed into the office, clambered over the desk, then through the hole and back to Carla's place, drywall dust raining down around them. With the sound of creaking wood echoing in his ears, Peter opened the front door and entered the stairwell first. The sense of *deja vu* was so strong, he felt dizzy.

Just above the last step, they stopped. Carla squeezed in next to him.

The room had undergone a drastic change since he'd last seen it. No more crashing waves inside the restaurant—just a flooded room filled with piles of seaweed, furniture, and waterlogged floorboards. The acrid air pressed in around him, stinking of decaying vegetation and the musty odor of mud overlaid with the sharp brine of salt water. The surf still pounded the ruined deck.

"What's that noise?" Lucas whispered.

Peter's eyebrows knit together, and his ears strained to hear over the sound of the surf. And then he heard it. A rustling. "It sounds like something is moving."

They didn't need their flashlights or Eric's camera. The watery light of dawn had arrived.

Peter focused his attention on the largest pile of seaweed directly across from them, between two tables lying on their sides. His stomach dropped. Something was moving underneath it. His eyes traveled to the next pile. It was moving too. The entire room suddenly seemed alive. Was it actually happening, or was he still feeling the effects of the pot?

A shadow loomed behind the glass front door. Behind Peter, Carla gasped. The figure resolved into a man of medium slim build, wearing a hooded jacket.

A fist pounded against the glass.

"Hey, Carla. You in there? Open up. There are more people coming, but you're stuck with me for now."

"It's Quint," Peter said. He wasn't surprised to see the firefighter. Quint practically lived at Carla's restaurant and had formed friendships with Carla and the locals who hung out there.

The seaweed piles shifted.

"He can't come in here," Carla hissed.

"Are the phones still out?" Peter asked.

Lucas checked his phone. "No signal."

"Who's that?" Natalie whispered behind them.

"It's Quint," Lucas replied. "He's a firefighter."

Natalie gave a little cry of relief. "Oh, thank God. He can help us."

A pile of seaweed toppled and fell into the pool of water beneath the floor joists, revealing a muscular black tentacle writhing just above the surface, its triangular end rotating like a radar antenna.

Peter's hair lifted on the back of his neck.

"If he comes in here he can't help us," Peter said, keeping his voice low.

Carla's nails dug into his arm.

They were in an impossible situation. Trapped in the stairwell without a way to warn Quint it was unsafe to enter the building, when that's exactly what he was trained and determined to do.

Peter guessed Quint had made his way over because resources were tight and the houses along Cortina Creek would get help first. Whoever was coordinating the disaster response couldn't know the waves had exploded through the floorboards and destabilized the buildings along the beach. They probably assumed anyone living there had received the emergency alert on their phones and evacuated.

There was no sign of the second creature, but that didn't mean it wasn't down there. With so much debris, it was impossible to tell what lurked in the depths below the joists. The one with the tentacle was deadly enough.

Quint disappeared, and for a moment, Peter thought he'd given up and left. But a few minutes later, he returned, carrying a log which he proceeded to bash against the glass. Jesus. Quint meant to break down the door.

"No, no, no," Carla muttered, covering her mouth with her hand as the commotion echoed through the stairwell.

The tentacle slapped the surface of the dark pool, sending a spray of water into the air.

"Quint, stop!" Yuki cried from the landing above them. "It's dangerous!"

"He can't hear us," Eric snapped.

Quint continued to strike the glass, each blow sending a shiver down Peter's spine. The door wouldn't hold for long. The floorboards were torn up all the way to the tiled entryway at the front door, and if Quint stepped on it, it would probably collapse under his weight.

Peter could see the creature slowly glide toward the door.

There was a loud crack and the sound of shattering glass. Quint used the end of the log to clear the shards from the edges of the doorframe, bent over, and stepped through.

And then Peter was shouting at him, voice hoarse. "Stop, Quint. Go back. The floor's gone. There's something in the water."

"Peter? What's going on?"

He could hear the confusion in Quint's voice.

Carla was bouncing on her feet, vibrating with anxiety. "The thing that killed Matt is in the water. We saw it." Her voice was shrill.

Peter had to see Quint to gauge his reaction. Clutching the railing with one hand, he leaned forward, one foot leaving the safety of the step, and peered around the wall.

Quint had retreated to the door, eyes sweeping across the room and taking in the destruction, his mouth slightly open. With a hood over his head, wearing faded jeans, he looked like a teenager.

"Are you kidding me?" Quint shouted. "What kind of thing are we talking about here?"

Natalie groaned in despair. "He doesn't believe us."

"We've seen it," Eric yelled. "Look, I'm a journalist, and I've got it all on camera. We don't know what it is, but you need to leave now!"

"And bring help!" Natalie shouted.

The water closest to the entrance rippled, lapping against the broken wooden joists once supporting the floor. Quint stared into the water, as if mesmerized.

In an explosion of water and debris, a long black arm shot into the air. It swayed like a dancer, moving with a sinuous grace toward its victim. Quint tensed, then turned, as if preparing to run, but it was too late. The stinger's tip glinted menacingly.

With astonishing speed, more of the tentacle pushed out of the water. It wound around Quint's torso and squeezed him like a giant python. Peter could see the surprise, then terror, in Quint's eyes as he grunted, clawing at the muscular coil, desperately struggling to free himself.

The stinger rose high into the air and, in one smooth, swift movement, swooped down and pierced Quint's neck, releasing a spray of dark, viscous ooze that splattered the white walls on either side of the door.

The firefighter screamed.

Never releasing its grip, the tentacle dragged Quint into the murky depths.

Chapter 33

48°

"Where's Lucas?" Carla gasped.

Peter looked around. Lucas had been right behind him when they fled up the stairs to Carla's apartment.

Panic rising, Peter poked his head into the bathroom. Lucas wasn't there. Or in the kitchen. Eric scrambled through the opening into Ken's apartment and returned, cursing, veins standing out on his neck.

"Did you leave him behind?" Yuki said in a low voice, staring at the door.

Peter's heart sank. He didn't want to enter the stairwell again. Ever, if possible. The walls pressing in around him. The choking claustrophobia. The fear of what waited below. But where else could Lucas be?

In the water. Stabbed by a tentacle.

Peter moved toward the door.

"I'll go with you," Eric said, crossing the room in several steps, hands balled into fists. He left his camera on the table.

Peter glanced over at Carla. She watched them, face flushed, breathing hard.

Eric unlocked the door but stepped aside to let Peter go first.

Pulse racing, Peter crept down the stairs. At the second landing, he spotted Lucas several steps below, crouching, his lean body pressed against the wall as if trying to make himself as small as possible. Peter's knees went weak with relief.

Standing, with the ceiling sloping downward and hindering his view, Peter couldn't see what commanded the young man's attention. Lucas hadn't seemed to hear their footsteps. Anything could be down there, just out of sight. Lucas could be engaged in a stare-off with a monster.

Peter had two choices: whisper Lucas's name or tap him on the shoulder and risk startling him. Lucas might yell. Loud noises were a bad idea.

"Lucas!" Eric whispered loudly. He sounded furious.

Lucas's head swiveled around. Holding a finger to his lips, he nodded, then crawled toward them. "There are lots of those things now. I counted eleven."

Peter's stomach dropped. Eleven. Two were bad enough. Eleven were terrifying. Scowling, he pointed up the stairs toward the door, but Lucas shook his head, his lips pressed together in a straight line of determination.

I want to see, he mouthed.

Peter stared at him through narrowed eyes, resentment bubbling up in his chest. Lucas's curiosity had put them in danger. Peter wanted to drag him upstairs, but he couldn't afford to make a racket, and he couldn't argue with him, not there.

He punched Lucas's arm to show him he wasn't happy. Lucas reared his head back in surprise, then scowled. A moment later, he swiveled on his knees and returned to the spot where they'd found him.

Peter glanced over his shoulder and saw Eric tiptoeing toward him, holding his camera. The reporter had gone back to get it.

A severe expression crossed Peter's face. No.

Eric shrugged, then pushed past him. The reporter wasn't as light on his feet as Lucas. The stairs creaked. Lucas's head whipped around, eyes snapping wide. He stood abruptly.

What happened next played out in slow motion.

Lucas lost his balance. His foot came down hard on the step below. There was a crack, and then his foot went through the middle of the board. With a yelp, he yanked it out and went sprawling backward to the floor at the bottom of the stairs. His weight was too much for the weakened wood. The floorboards snapped, plunging Lucas into the water below.

Later, Peter couldn't remember how he'd reached the last safe step or when Carla had joined him, but suddenly, they were both there, gazing into the black pool and willing Lucas to emerge.

And then he surfaced, gasping for breath, hands clawing the water. Peter didn't know if Lucas could swim, but it didn't look like it. If it had been the beach and Lucas had been a swimmer in trouble, Peter wouldn't have hesitated. He would have jumped into the surf to save him.

But this wasn't the ocean. It was a hole filled with muddy salt water, debris, and creatures with tentacles that had killed four people. Chances were, if he went in, he wouldn't make it out again. But it was Lucas, and Peter couldn't leave him to die.

He was taking off his jacket when Carla grabbed his arm. "No! He's got it. He's almost here."

Carla was so fixated on Lucas, struggling toward them, she didn't see the ripple behind him. The creature with the face poked its head out of the water, then disappeared. A moment later, a long, muscular body—a strange translucent red—broke the surface less than a yard away. Then off to the right, closer to the front door, two sleek backs appeared to be swimming in a circle around a floating trash can draped with seaweed.

It seemed to Peter as though the creatures were waiting for something. But for what? There was no time to contemplate their motivations. Peter grabbed the railing with one hand, leaned forward as far as he dared, and reached out with his other. His fingers brushed Lucas's shirt, and then he had him. Chest heaving with exertion, Peter dragged the young man out of the water to safety.

"Go!" Peter shouted at Lucas, pushing him toward the stairs.

Carla screamed.

Peter's heart went off like a cherry bomb in his chest. The creature with the face reared up from the water. Peter could see the rest of it now. Fish didn't have necks, he thought to himself, yet his mind struggled to apply one to the space below the strange, human-like features that were all wrong and terrifying. No chin, no neck. Just a sleek, dark column of flesh.

The face hovered there, considering him with an intense gaze. And then it blinked. And blinked again. It had a nictitating membrane, like a shark. The creature was upright and swaying from side to side.

It launched itself into the air, landing half on, half off the bottom step, the rest of its muscular body thrashing wildly and sending up a spray of water. It had a small, ugly puckered mouth edged in black. Even if it had teeth, could it open its mouth wide enough to do any serious damage?

In moments, Peter had the answer.

With a sharp click, the thing unhinged its jaw. Its mouth yawned open, stretching impossibly wide. The gaping hole revealed a short row of sharp, jagged teeth and, beyond it, more teeth shaped like small, deadly scythes.

The creature was so fixed on Peter, it didn't seem to notice Carla's desperate attempt to grab the phone receiver dangling just out of her reach. As the freakish mouth opened wider, Carla's fingers closed around the receiver. With astonishing speed, Carla brought her arm in a circle above her head and bashed it against the creature's head.

The result was immediate.

The blow had stunned it. Its eyes lost focus, and it was listing to the side.

With a cry, Carla brought the receiver down on the back of its head again. The creature tipped sideways into the water.

Carla held the receiver over her head. Glaring at the water, she bellowed, "Any other motherfuckers out there care for a little of this?"

"Carla, go!" Peter hauled Carla up the stairs, strengthened by the first, tiny sign of hope that they might survive after all.

Chapter 34

breezy

Carla could have pounded Lucas with the phone if she hadn't been so relieved he was still alive. Wet, shivering, and numb…but alive. She still couldn't believe he'd almost gotten himself killed, all because his curiosity had overcome his good sense.

She went into the bathroom and, out of habit, hit the light switch. *Duh.* The electricity had been out for hours.

Thankful for gas water heaters, she ran a bath half full of tepid water and ordered Lucas to get in it. He smelled like brine and fish. Lucas was too stunned to notice or protest when Carla dumped a generous amount of lavender-and-eucalyptus-scented Epsom salt into the tub.

She went into the kitchen, returned with a plastic trash bag, and dropped it into the sink. "Stick your dirty clothes in here."

"Then I won't have anything to wear." His thin chest appeared caved in. His breath was uneven.

Carla pointed at the tub. "Don't worry about it. I'll figure something out."

She could feel the adrenaline moving through her body, still too hyped up to sit down or even to cry over Quint. Carla had to keep moving. Distract herself. If she slowed down, she'd have time to think about everything they'd been through in the last eight hours. Including the wet thud of the telephone receiver smacking the creature with the face. Its head had a disgusting meaty texture that made her stomach clench just thinking about it.

After everyone rehashed the horrific scene that had played out below, not once but several times, the group fell into an uneasy, wary silence. Peter paced in front of the patio door. The weak light of dawn bathed the room in a watery light.

"This is insane!" Natalie wailed. "I just want to get out of here!"

Carla stationed herself outside the bathroom, splitting her attention between Lucas and the others. He might be an adult, but after nearly drowning in a pool infested with demon fish, he seemed willing to follow her orders like a child, contrite after misbehaving. Carla could hear the splash of water through the door.

"The building is falling down, and she wants him to take a bath," Natalie said. She sat on the couch, clutching a pillow to her stomach.

Yuki reached into the hall closet where Carla kept extra towels. "He'll hurry. Besides, what's the rush? We still don't know how we're getting out of here." She went into the bedroom and Carla heard the opening and closing of drawers.

"If we ever get out," Eric mumbled. "Look what happened to the one guy who tried to rescue us."

"At least we know how to stun them," Yuki said. "Thanks to Carla."

Peter cleared his throat. "True. But I doubt any of us want to get close enough to one of those things to try."

"Still, it's useful to know that works," Eric said. "That's how fishermen kill fish. They bonk them."

Natalie snorted. "Really? That's what it's called? Bonking fish?"

"I'm serious. That's what they call it. Look it up if you don't believe me."

Natalie glanced down at her phone. "I would. Still no signal. If we could only call someone and tell them what's going on, they could send a rescue helicopter or something."

"I can think of a giant tentacle that might take that as a fun challenge." Peter gave a grim laugh.

Yuki handed Carla a stack of clothes atop a towel. Carla eyed them, then nodded in approval. How the woman was still functioning after everything she'd been through, Carla had no idea. Maybe, like her, Yuki was grateful for something useful to do.

She took the pair of old blue sweats and over-sized flannel shirt from Yuki and, eyes averted, shoved them through the opening in the bathroom door.

"I'm scared," Yuki said.

Tears, unbidden, sprang to Carla's eyes. "I am too."

Behind them, there was a thud, quickly followed by a grunt of surprise. Carla's stomach dropped. Now what?

There was something outside the patio door.

Correction. *Someone.*

It was Amalia. Peter rushed to the door, unlocked it, and pulled her inside. Eric slammed it shut.

"How the hell did you get here?" Peter stuttered.

Amalia's apartment was at the far end of the row of buildings, closest to the creek and pier. There was no ledge between Ken's place and hers. Unless she could scale the sides of buildings, Carla did not understand how Amalia had made it to her balcony.

Amalia scanned the room, taking in the group, eyes going wide at the crumbling walls. She was her usual elegant, put-together self, dressed in faded jeans, a white turtleneck, and a windbreaker. Amalia was tall, with freckles across her nose and hair the color of pearls. Before Jacob had died in an accident involving one of Amalia's chartered boats, she and Carla had been good friends.

Carla knew it was unfair and probably cruel to cut off Amalia the way she had. But all she felt was rage whenever she saw her, and she'd lacked the energy to explore it with her therapist. All her strength had gone into pulling herself out of the black hole that was her life without Jacob in it. Amalia had been a casualty, a relationship she'd intended to repair. She just hadn't gotten around to it yet.

The number of people in her life had dwindled after Jacob's death, and she only had herself to blame.

After Peter quickly introduced Eric and Natalie, Carla stepped toward Amalia. The woman flinched a little. Up close, Carla could see the details she'd missed. Amalia had dark circles under her eyes. Since she'd last seen her, the hair around Amalia's face had gone from platinum to nearly white. There were more fine wrinkles around her eyes too.

"How did you get here?"

Amalia lifted her hand, index finger pointing upward. "I came over the roof."

Chapter 35

light mist

Everyone crowded around Amalia, talking breathlessly about the monsters, the buildings, and the storm. Carla moved them aside because she had questions.

"What do you mean you came over the roof? How?"

Amalia glanced at Eric's laptop screen, frozen on a picture of the first creature they'd seen swimming in the restaurant.

She rubbed the side of her face. "So, you've seen them." She exhaled loudly. "Good. I thought I was going to have to tell you about them, and I didn't think you'd believe me. This makes it easier.

"I've been watching them. There are some of those things in the creek, and I saw one under the pier. My front door's on the ocean side of the building, so my stairs are—or were—connected to the deck. They're completely gone now, so I was trying to figure out how to get down to the street when I saw one of those things grab someone who was inspecting the bridge. After that, there was no way I was going to hang out on my balcony and start yelling for help, luring rescuers to their deaths. And then I remembered the hatches up to the roof. There's one in every other building. There's one between you and Ken."

"Ken's dead," Lucas announced, entering the room. His hair was wet, but he was clean, and he'd lost the dazed expression.

Amalia clapped a hand over her mouth.

Carla shook her head. "It wasn't those things. He had a diabetic episode and never came out of it."

Amalia gave a tired sigh. "What a night."

"What a night," Carla repeated.

The two women stared at each other. All the anger Carla had felt for the woman drained out of her, and she felt lighter. There was only one thing left to do.

"I'm sorry," Carla said in a low voice. "About everything. I just...I can be a bitch sometimes."

Amalia made a dismissive sound, shrugging away Carla's apology with a wave of her hand, but Carla could see the faint shimmer of tears in her eyes.

There was so much they didn't know.

Of the eleven creatures Lucas had counted, how many of them had tentacles bristling with poison-spiked stingers? How many had mouths that could expand, exposing two sets of razor-sharp teeth? They acted like predators, but they'd also exhibited inconsistent and puzzling behavior. Sometimes hanging back and watching, other times attacking without warning, unprovoked.

Carla half listened to Peter and Amalia comparing notes. Amalia knew more about fish than anyone else in the group, and Peter was keen to hear her take on things. Not that she had anything particularly insightful to share. She was just as baffled as the rest of them.

Carla was more concerned about making it across the roof to Amalia's before the building came tumbling down. The structure shuddered and shook every time the staircase to the vacation rental swung and smashed into the wall, and Carla could feel the vibrations through her feet.

"Hey, folks, let's finish this conversation someplace safer, shall we?" Carla peered out the sliding door at the open hatch in the eaves.

A retractable ladder reached down to the patio, with a second hatch in the roof above. Easy enough to climb up and onto the roof, as long as no corpses came flying their way.

Peter insisted on standing guard and going last.

The worst of the storm was over, but the breeze still whipped up whitecaps on the ocean, a mass of choppy waves brown with mud from the swollen creek.

Carla stared at him, hands on hips. "And what are you going to do if you see one of those things?" she asked as Lucas shimmied up the rungs.

Peter stepped over to the door leading into the kitchen and grabbed a chair. "I'll chuck one of these at it."

Lucas disappeared onto the roof. A moment later, his head appeared in the hatch, and he beckoned her up.

She climbed as fast as she could, heart thudding. Peter winced with every careful step up the rungs, and only when he was finally standing safe beside her did Carla realize she'd been holding her breath during his ascent.

The drizzle had turned into a light mist. The cold morning air, thick with moisture, felt good on her face. Seagulls wheeled and screeched overhead. When a splat of poop just missed them, Carla gave a giddy laugh.

The roof was flat, except for the western edge, which sloped downward. The building underneath shook as the loose stairs banged into it.

They stepped around pools of water to join the others. Eric was wearing his backpack, camera on his shoulder. He was already recording. To Carla's surprise, Natalie was describing the scene for the camera and doing an excellent job of it too.

The sky was still an ominous gray. To the north, a line of rain clouds hovered over the San Refugio hills. Palm trees swayed in the wind.

Carla's eyes fell on the disaster below, and she gasped.

The water had receded from Ocean View Drive. Mud covered the length of the street. Waves had pushed benches, trash bins, patio tables, chairs, and umbrellas into the road, along with logs, tree branches, and garbage. The steps to the bandshell had disappeared under an enormous pile of driftwood, At the far end of the street, a small blue car lay on its side.

"Shit," Lucas said.

The buildings opposite—a mix of shops, restaurants, and houses—sat at a slightly higher elevation. Debris littered the sidewalks, but the doors and windows were still intact. There was no sign of any people.

Despite the destruction, the quaint village possessed a mournful beauty. Behind the brightly colored stucco and Victorian gingerbread was a tough foundation and strong bones. The streets were a mess, but the town's spirit was intact.

"What time is it?" Natalie asked. "Shouldn't help be here already?"

The power was still out. Not a single light shone behind the windows.

"They must have closed all the roads into the village," Peter said. "To keep out the lookie-loos."

Natalie frowned. "I used to work in TV news before going into PR. This doesn't make any sense. Where are the

TV crews? You'd think they'd be here to do live shots for their morning shows. This is a big story."

Eric scoffed. "San Refugio isn't a big city like San Francisco, and since we don't have a cell down here, we can't contact anyone or share pictures on social media. How is anyone supposed to know what happened?"

"I guess." Natalie still sounded uncertain. "But where are all the people?"

Peter cleared his throat. "Most of the houses around here are second homes, so they're empty during the week. The place is pretty dead this time of year. Folks living next to the creek were smart enough to evacuate. There were only two of us at the condos yesterday."

Carla's eyebrows shot up at Peter's abrupt change in tone. "Maggie?"

Peter sighed. He leaned toward her and lowered his voice. "Yeah. Last night, I was sure it was the storm that killed her. But now, I think we can guess what really happened." He sighed again. "Jesus. I hope she's still where I left her."

"What do you—"

Carla was interrupted by a panicked yell from Lucas. While the group was staring straight ahead at the heart of the village, Lucas was facing the pier.

"What the fuck?" he shouted.

Time seemed to slow as Carla spun around. She felt a rush of goosebumps raise on her arms and at the nape of her neck. Carla heard Peter's swift intake of breath and Yuki's and Natalie's startled cries. Something hit her ankle and bounced away. Eric's microphone. She was hardly aware of the pain.

At the far end of the damaged pier, pushing up from the chaotic sea, something was moving. Something enormous— a strange and otherworldly shade of dark green. Several tentacles, large enough to be seen without binoculars. They glistened and pulsed in the gray light of morning, slithering smoothly and silently over a railing. Exploring. Seeking.

A wave of nausea rose in Carla's throat, forcing bile into her mouth. Suddenly dizzy, she swayed, overcome with panic. The ordinary world had no place for such monstrous things, and yet, a primitive part of her mind stirred with recognition. A dark mirror of the ancient past when strange life forms slithered out of the water.

The wind whispered eerily through the dry fronds of a palm tree on the street below.

Lucas was shouting again. "Look! A drone."

A dark shape appeared over the cliff and made straight for the ruined pier.

Peter scanned the bluff overlooking the beach. "I can't see the operator."

The drone's movements were erratic. Up, down, sideways. Natalie and Lucas waved their hands in the air, shouting as though the drone could hear. Eric fumbled with his camera and cursed.

Knuckles pressed against her forehead, Yuki repeated, "Over here. We're over here," with the intensity of an incantation.

Only Carla stood silent, frozen, as if the appearance of the abomination at the end of the pier had numbed her.

The drone whizzed through the air, away from them and toward the creature.

And then the tentacles were gone.

A siren wailed in the distance.

Chapter 36

51°

Peter guessed the fire truck had parked several blocks away, probably near the library. The crews would arrive soon enough, and that didn't give them much time. A conversation was in order, and that wasn't going to be easy after what they'd just seen. Lucas and Natalie were walking in circles, hands stuck in their hair, babbling in an endless loop of disbelief. Yuki stared out into the street, watching for help to arrive, bouncing on the balls of her feet in anticipation. Eric stared at his camera as if it had betrayed him. He hadn't managed to turn it on in time to capture the monster.

Peter wished Lucas and Natalie would shut up. He moved away behind a vent so he could think, pulling Carla along with him. Her stunned expression still hadn't left her face.

She looked up at him, blinking. "What?"

"We need to figure out what we're going to say when they get here."

She pressed a finger between her eyes, staring off into space. "Why don't we just tell them what happened?"

"They're not going to believe us."

"They'll have to. You worked with those guys. They know you."

Peter rubbed the side of his face. "Not so much anymore. Some of the guys left. A few retired, like me. There's a lot of new guys I've never met. If I start talking about monsters in the water, they'll think I'm crazy."

"But…," Carla stuttered. She pointed at the pier. "The drone must have been taking video. Other people will see it. And what about what happened to Matt and the other guy? Something killed them, and now we know what it is. We'll just tell them. They'll have to believe us."

Peter shook his head. "Maybe. Maybe not. Come on. How would you react if you were sitting in a city council meeting and Joe Blow steps up to the mic and says he saw something crazy in the water at San Refugio Beach and he wants you to do something about it?"

He waited, arms folded across his chest. When she bit her lip, and looked away, he continued.

"Get my point?

"I guess," Carla finally said. "Then what are we supposed to do?"

Is this what professional pilots experienced after spotting a UFO? How many times had the fear of derision silenced eyewitnesses to events the world needed to know about? His only comfort—a small one—was that Carla and the others had seen them too. He hoped the first responders had seen or heard about these nasty creatures. Fire and police radios worked even if the cell towers were down. Maybe the things had shown up on other beaches too. Maybe they weren't isolated to San Refugio, so the firefighters would believe Peter when he warned them. But he couldn't count on that.

Their raised voices brought the others over.

"You're not going to let them go inside, are you?" Natalie said.

Peter cleared his throat. "I'm not sure I can stop them."

Yuki moved to stand in front of him, so close he could feel her breath on his face. "You have to try. You can't just let them…die."

Lucas rolled his eyes. "Are you guys forgetting Eric got video? It's on his computer. All he has to do is show them. If they see for themselves, they'll believe it."

"I'm not showing that video to anyone except my news director," Eric said. "They might try and confiscate my camera. My computer. No way."

"They won't do that." Peter's voice betrayed his uncertainty.

Lucas's mouth dropped open. He threw his hands into the air. "Eric, you *have* to show them. People could *die* if you don't."

"I don't *have* to do anything." Eric clutched his camera a little tighter. "You don't understand."

Natalie scoffed. "You don't know what you're talking about. They only confiscate footage if they think it shows evidence of a crime. You just don't want to show them. You're an asshole."

Eric shrugged. "You can call me whatever you want, I'm not showing the video to anyone except my boss." He hesitated. "Look, if I play the video, you can bet whoever sees it is going to whip out their phone and take pictures of my screen, and then he's going to send it to all his buddies. The next thing you know, it's all over the place. Without context or background information from marine biologists…or any of the things people will need to hear before they can understand what happened. Hell, we don't even understand what happened yet. So no, nobody sees my video."

"You're an even bigger asshole than I thought," Natalie snapped.

"And the video is the property of the TV station. It's not mine to give away," Eric said stubbornly. "You said you used to work in TV. You should know that."

Peter wished he could convince Eric to show his video to the authorities, but the reporter did have a point. And who's to say their rescuers would even take the time to look at it?

Amalia had watched the entire exchange with fixed attention but remained quiet. Peter wondered what that was about. Amalia was an experienced sea captain and not shy with her opinions. She obviously had one, by the way the muscles in her face locked into a steely mask.

Tired of the argument, Peter walked to the far side of the roof, his back turned to the others. He surveyed the pier, wondering where the tentacles had gone. Hopefully, back to the bay, to the open ocean, eventually disappearing forever into the depths of the Monterey Submarine Canyon.

An excited whoop broke through his dark thoughts.

"Someone's coming," Lucas yelled.

Peter hurried over as Natalie jumped up and down. "Hello! We're up here!" She grabbed Lucas's arm and gave it a gleeful shake. "I just want to get the hell out of here."

Lucas rubbed his stomach. "I could totally use a steak quesadilla."

Their desperate tone wasn't lost on Peter. He peered over the ledge. A man in a black lieutenant's uniform looked up at him. A flush of heat burned Peter's neck and face. He'd rescued plenty of people in his role as a state lifeguard, but he'd never needed rescuing himself. It just added to the unreality of the moment.

Peter recognized the man. Ryan Jones. His squinty eyes were set in a fleshy face that was at odds with his thin, bony body.

Peter managed a sheepish wave. "Hey, Jonesy."

"Hey, yourself." Jones had a deep, throaty voice. "I've got two more guys on the way. How many of you are there?"

"Seven. Are there just the three of you?"

Jones sucked in his considerable cheeks. "For now. The storm gave the hills a good whomping. Cars trapped in underpasses, major accidents on the highway, trees down everywhere. We're expecting help from outside agencies, but it'll be a while. The rest of my guys are at a mobile home park. A bunch of redwoods came down, wiped out an entire family. We've still got eight missing."

Behind him, Natalie groaned. "What about us?"

Peter ignored her, all his attention focused on the man below.

Jones scratched his neck. "Have you seen Quint? He signed up to do a first pass down here, but we haven't heard from him."

Peter could feel the others staring at him. Carla squeezed his arm.

"Quint was here." His voice was thick with gloom.

The lieutenant's eyes snapped open. "Whoa. I don't like the sound of that."

Peter recalled Quint's final moments, eyes bulging in terror as the stinger pierced his neck. The young man's screams still echoed in his head.

Jones scowled. "Then where is he?"

The words dried up in his throat. Peter swallowed hard and ran his tongue around his lips. They were cracked and tasted like salt water. Jones stared up at him expectantly.

Peter finally managed to get the words out. "He's dead."

Chapter 37

light winds

When Peter asked the fire lieutenant to fetch a ladder so they could get off the roof and talk more easily, Jones refused. "First, I need to know what happened to my guy."

Peter did his best. It seemed wrong to shout that kind of thing. When he was done, his voice was hoarse, and he didn't know if the distance separating them had made it easier or harder to break that kind of news.

"You saw it? You saw it happen?" Jones kept repeating. His brows lowered, and his chin jutted out.

The other two firefighters joined him on the sidewalk.

Peter had chosen his words carefully. No mention of "monster" or "creature." Nothing that could trigger disbelief.

Knowing what he knew and carefully doling it out in bits and pieces was exhausting. Peter let out a heavy sigh. "I don't know what it was. Maybe a big ray of some sort. It had a tentacle and a stinger. It came out of the water, stung him, and pulled him in."

"You think it's still in there?" Jones took a step back and glanced warily in the direction of the restaurant. "We need to clear the building."

"Nothing to clear," Peter said hurriedly. "I've already explained. Ken Bigg is dead in his apartment, and a tourist named Olivia Watson is also accounted for because we saw her body. You need to wait for backup before you go inside. There's no one else in the buildings."

Jones shook his head. "You can't know that for sure. We need to take a look ourselves. The building on the end over there looks unstable. We can't wait around. And police and sheriffs got their hands full elsewhere."

Blood pounded in Peter's ears. He wanted Jones to wait. Wait until police arrived with firepower. But firefighters weren't trained to wait. They were trained to act.

Peter stretched out his hands wide, then relaxed them. He did it several times, drawing in his breath and releasing it before speaking. "As I said, the floor's gone in the two restaurants. You'd have to hop from joist to joist, and there's so much water, it's like an aquarium, except the water is full of debris and you won't be able to see what's down there."

Amalia walked up, clearing her throat. She held out her phone. "My business is next to the creek. I took a picture from my apartment at first light. It's not great, but you'll be able to see why Peter is so concerned about your safety."

Peter moved the phone in front of his face and studied it. It showed a dark hump cresting out of the water. Several yards behind it, a muscular tentacle snaked in the air. Peter's jaw clenched so hard it sent ripples of pain up to his ears.

Jones removed his jacket and stretched it out like an old-fashioned life net. "All right. Let's take a look. Drop it here. And try not to miss."

Amalia released the phone. Jones snatched it before it could bounce to the ground.

They watched as he bent over the screen, head rearing back in surprise.

Jones looked up at Amalia, blinking. "Did you Photoshop that?"

"Of course not," Amalia said curtly. "I'd need electricity for that, and it's been out since the storm started."

"That could be a dolphin," Jones said. "Or an orca. I take my boat out every weekend, and there's a lot of both out there."

Amalia snorted. "Neither have tentacles."

"That could be something else." Jones pocketed the phone. "Honestly, it looks like bull kelp to me, sticking up out of the water."

"Oh, it does, does it?" Amalia sneered. "I own San Refugio Boat Charters, and I know the bay like the back of my hand. I can tell you that is *not* bull kelp."

Jones pushed his shoulders back and raised his hands in the air, fingers spread wide. "All right. Thank you, ma'am, for showing us your photo. I appreciate it." Shifting his gaze to Peter, his manner turned brusque. "And I appreciate the words of warning. But I need to see for myself what we're dealing with and make my own assessment. Now if I can please ask for your patience, hang up there a little while longer, and we'll take it from here."

"At least bring us down first," Peter shouted.

Icy blue eyes regarded him with professional detachment. "Considering what you just said, sounds like you'll be safer up there, out of harm's way. We won't be long."

Peter couldn't be sure, but the lieutenant seemed to be smirking. His face felt like it was on fire. He'd been dismissed. His years of experience counted for nothing. He might as well have been an old surfer, trying to tell the professionals how to do their jobs. Jesus.

"You're making a big mistake," Amalia said coldly, then turned on her heel. Before she walked away, she patted Peter's arm. "We tried."

Peter's body drooped with defeat and exhaustion.

The firefighters moved swiftly, grabbing their equipment and jogging toward Carla's restaurant. They stopped just outside the busted-out door and conferred among themselves. The two other men were younger than Jones by at least a decade. One had a handlebar mustache; the other had a shaved head. Peter couldn't hear what they were saying. Jones glanced up, and their eyes locked for an awkward moment. Peter thought he detected a hint of uncertainty in those squinty eyes.

He hoped so.

Peter shook his head. Called, "Don't do it." One final, useless warning. His legs wanted to run toward the group. His arms wanted to pull them back, away from the waiting, black water. His mouth wanted to open wide and scream, "Stop!"

Instead, he did nothing. Cold waves of foreboding washed over him.

The firefighter with the shaved head shot Peter a pitiful smile and turned again to face the restaurant, kicking aside a small pile of debris.

There was so much he hadn't told them. Like the water-logged landing giving way beneath Lucas. The way he'd fallen into the murky water. The menace and intelligence in the creature's eyes. The way Carla had bashed the thing on the back of the head, again and again. But Jones had been visibly impatient the longer Peter talked, so he'd kept it short.

Realizing nothing more could be done, Peter watched.

"We can't see what's going on from here," Eric said. His voice betrayed the first sign of anxiety about the danger the three firefighters faced.

Yuki pointed west. "If we move over there, we'll have a better view."

Peter followed her finger. She was right. The building was shaped like a semi-circle. They moved closer to the west end of the building. The action was farther away, but they could now see the sidewalk and the three men. Eric lifted his camera into position and began recording.

They were just in time to see Jones raise a foot over the threshold, elbows at his side to avoid the shattered glass around the door frame. He turned slightly and waved his hand at the other firefighters to stay back. And then he stepped inside and disappeared.

Peter's heart began to beat wildly. That's all he needed. To keel over from a heart attack at this moment, of all moments. He wiped his sweaty palms on his jeans.

Peter squeezed his eyes shut, imagining Jones sweeping his flashlight from one side of the cavernous space to the other. Carla leaned against him, breathing raggedly.

"You seeing anything?" Handlebar Mustache yelled.

Peter's heart sank. That was another thing he hadn't warned them about. The damn things were sensitive to sound. The guy might as well have rung a dinner bell.

From inside the restaurant, Jones screamed.

Chapter 38

thinning clouds

The two firefighters on the sidewalk seemed frozen by whatever they were seeing. Inside, Jones continued to scream, his unintelligible cries blending with the shrieks of seagulls circling overhead in the dreary sky.

The bald man snapped out of his paralysis and lunged toward the door. He reached the entrance but then pulled back. A long, dark, glistening arm shot out, encircled his waist, and dragged him through the doorway.

A screech ripped through the air, then a high-pitched, wavering yell of, "Noooo," before it abruptly stopped.

Beside Peter, Yuki moaned, and Carla cried out, her sharp fingernails pressing through the fabric of his jacket and digging into his skin.

The mustached firefighter recoiled in horror. He stumbled back and began pacing in a frantic circle, hands pressed against the sides of his head.

Recalling the enormity of the tentacle they'd spotted at the dock, Peter shouted, "Get back! Get back!"

The others joined in, a chorus of panicked voices warning against the creatures hidden in the depths.

Their voices finally seemed to break through his daze. He glanced toward them just as a figure staggered out of the building. It was Jones lurching forward, barely able to stay on his feet.

He turned toward them, maybe attracted by their cries of alarm, revealing the ghastliness of his injury. Blood smeared his skin and clothes. A gruesome, vertical gash ran from his ribcage to his crotch. Both hands were desperately trying to push his glistening insides back into his body.

Jones was halfway to being gutted, cleaned like a fish.

He pitched forward, unable to break his momentum with his hands filled with guts. His knees struck the ground first. His head followed, cracking against an iron grate.

Jones toppled over, intestines spilling from the bloody gash.

The firefighter with the mustache whipped off his jacket and pressed it into Jones's stomach. He was trying to roll Jones onto his back when a dark blur appeared.

The grate. It was connected to the cavernous space below her restaurant.

"Watch out!" Carla ran along the edge of the roof.

The tentacle unfurled slowly, almost lazily, and pushed into the air, its point end quivering.

The man working on Jones seemed oblivious to the danger…and to their warning cries. To Peter, it felt like an eternity before the mustached firefighter finally looked up. The stinger came slashing down, barely missing its target. He fell onto his butt and scuttled back. The tentacle flicked upward once more and hovered menacingly, its stinger rotating.

"Don't move!" Peter yelled, his voice thick with desperation.

But staying still defied the human instinct to flee in the face of danger. The firefighter continued to scoot backward, his heavy boots dragging against the pavement.

The stinger whipped through the air again, striking the man in the neck with such force, it tore through one side and out the other. Blood spurted from his neck and mouth, and he toppled over. The slimy limb wriggled frantically, desperate to be released from its fleshy prison. And then it ripped through the terrible, ragged hole it had made in the man's neck.

The firefighter with the handlebar mustache was dead. Jones, however, was now struggling to raise his head.

A flash of movement. Peter's eyes widened in confusion. A dark shape seemed to arrive out of nowhere, landing on Jones, flattening him to the iron grate.

"The fuck!" Lucas yelled into his ear.

It was the bald firefighter, clothes soaking and ripped to shreds, legs entangled in ropey seaweed. His face was mostly gone—an oval expanse of mangled, bloody flesh, his scalp gouged and grooved, chunks missing.

The impact of the human missile was too much for Jones. His leg twitched and then went still.

The three men who had come to rescue them from the ravages of the storm lay dead, themselves ravaged by the monsters the storm had brought ashore.

Chapter 39

53°

There was no night, no mist, no blanket to obscure the carnage. The morning light, though dreary, was unforgiving.

Carla was sick of death. Sick of being trapped. Sick of being scared. And now, the east side of the building was listing dangerously, creaking and shuddering. Yuki and Natalie wept quietly. Lucas sat cross-legged in a puddle of water, head in hands. Peter roused them and brought the shocked group to the west side of the roof, as far away as they could get from the gory scene and the end of the building that seemed sure to crumble.

Eric had set aside his camera and crouched next to Lucas, patting his back.

Peter and Amalia stood slightly apart, talking in urgent tones, the tension between them as thick as the humidity from the storm.

Carla studied them and rubbed her face. It felt grimy, like the rest of her. Her underarms were sticky with sweat. If she weren't outside in the cold, breezy sea air, she would probably reek. A hot shower wouldn't wash away the horrors she'd witnessed, but she desperately longed for one anyway.

Amalia scoffed. "And what do you think *Carla* is going to think of that?"

Frowning, Carla hurried over. "What am I gonna think about what?"

Before Peter could reply, Amalia said, "Peter says we can't afford to wait for more help, and he has an idea about how we can kill those things ourselves, but I said we should ask you first because—"

"Because there's a slight chance it might take out your restaurant and maybe even the entire building," Peter said, voice flat. "But I don't think so."

Carla's eyes snapped wide. Suddenly, she felt very awake. "How?"

"We'll blow those things up." Peter cleared his throat.

"Maybe," Amalia said. "If you can hit one. It's a long shot, in my opinion."

"What the hell are you guys talking about? Can someone explain?" Carla clenched her teeth so hard it sent a stab of pain shooting up her jaw.

Peter glanced at the others before speaking. "Sorry. Here's the plan. Now that the water has receded from the street, we can get out through a front window in Amalia's apartment…"

"We'd break our legs!" Carla protested.

When Amalia had sold her house in the hills, she'd spent big bucks renovating her office space, raising the ceiling to hang vintage skiffs and surfboards from the beams. The changes meant the bottom floor of the apartment sat high above the street. Too high.

Peter shook his head. "We can do it. I have an idea. It's those things in the water I'm worried about. Lucas said he counted eleven of them in your place alone. There's probably more in Yuki's restaurant. We need to kill them while we can before they swim back out to the bay. I'm not sure if you noticed because there's so much junk bobbing around, but there are at least a half dozen propane tanks in there from the heaters on the back deck." He hesitated, cleared his throat again. "Amalia says her son keeps his rifles in her apartment…"

"Axel was part of his high school rifle team, and he had to leave them behind when he went to college."

Peter scowled at the interruption. "The rifles have scopes, so we don't have to get too close. I have some road flares in my truck. We light those, throw them into the water, and see if we can shoot the tanks. Hopefully, it will work like I think it will, and that will cause the propane tanks to heat up and explode." Peter flicked his fingers in the air. "Boom."

Carla didn't know what she was expecting, but it wasn't that. "Boom" could only mean one thing. Her restaurant, her business, her livelihood, going up in flames. She owned the building. Her insurance was good, but she didn't have to check the policy to know it wouldn't pay out if the company discovered she had intentionally blown up the place.

Although, if she wasn't the one to pull the trigger, that would make her a victim. And Peter an arsonist.

What the hell was she thinking? Those were just dumb, minor details. If they allowed those things to escape—free to terrorize all the communities dotting the Monterey Bay—she'd have no business. No one would have a business because no one in their right mind would ever choose to come to San Refugio again. Her property would be worthless. Better it gets blown up than let the monsters live another day.

Her stomach fluttered. She gave a curt nod. "Okay. Are you that good of a shot?" She directed her question at Peter.

"No." Peter didn't hesitate. "But Yuki is."

"Yuki?" Carla hissed. The last time Yuki had held a gun, it had been a disaster.

"Axel and Yuki would go shooting sometimes. He says she's a damn good shot," Amalia said in a low voice. "Better than him, even, and that's saying a lot."

Carla glanced at Yuki, staring off into the distance. Her face was pale and devoid of expression. Yuki had lost her husband less than twenty-four hours before and survived a horrific night. Was she up to the task? The success of the plan relied on a woman whose hands trembled as she pushed a strand of dark hair away from her face. The woman who'd cost them the only two weapons they had.

Carla jerked her head in Yuki's direction. "Well. Let's ask her."

Chapter 40

tide 2.7 ft

The east side of the building creaked and groaned behind them. They hurried across the width of the roof toward Amalia's apartment with purpose and grim determination. The plan seemed to cheer everyone up, especially Lucas and Natalie, who bounded ahead like teenagers headed to their first nightclub. The past tension between them seemed forgotten. Carla watched with a mix of surprise and envy. Adult worries about all that could go wrong robbed her of such optimism.

"I think they've seen too many movies," Peter muttered.

The plan also seemed to have a rejuvenating effect on Yuki. "Matt would want me to do this," she said before striding briskly forward, lips pressed together.

Carla just prayed Yuki didn't lose her confidence at the critical moment.

But first, they had to get out of the building, and that part of the plan depended on Lucas and Eric.

Natalie nervously peered over the edge of the roof. "Is there water in your place?" she asked Amalia. "They could be in there, waiting for us to come down."

Amalia gave a stiff nod. "The back of the office is almost completely submerged, but there's less water near the street side, and the windows are still intact, so we should be able to get out the front without a problem." She paused. "I hope."

Natalie shifted uneasily. "That's great."

Peter insisted on going down the ladder to Amalia's balcony first. Carla was relieved his back didn't seem to be

213

bothering him, something she attributed to all the adrenaline coursing through his veins. But Peter still seemed jittery after the bloodbath they'd witnessed, his eyes darting around as if he expected a giant tentacle to come slithering over the balcony rail.

He made them wait several minutes, checking for signs of the creatures below before he beckoned them down. Lucas went next. His pants were soaked through, but his feet seemed to barely touch the rungs. Eric followed more slowly as he managed his backpack, made heavy by his laptop and video camera.

Carla went last. Before she descended, she stared out at the gray sea. The storm had thinned, but the waves were still unrelenting, ferocious, and frothing as they climbed up the beach. With the king tide past its peak and the winds calmer, the water level had dropped enough to see glimpses of damaged wooden decks between the ebb and flow of the surf.

Amalia's apartment was just as Carla remembered it. Her last visit had been just days before the fateful boat trip that killed her son and ten other teenagers. She and Amalia had sat in the living room with a view of the ocean and the pier, drinking white wine, laughing, and watching the sunset, blissfully unaware tragedy awaited.

High soaring ceilings. Cream-colored leather couches and chairs. Pillows and throws in browns and grays. It was a beautiful, restful place.

Lucas whistled. "Whoa. Fancy."

Natalie poked her head into a room off the hallway. "I'd kill to have a bathroom like this."

Amalia nodded distractedly and ran up the stairs to the second floor. At the top, she stopped and pointed at Lucas. "Don't sit down on my sofa, young man. Not in those wet clothes. Come on up here. Axel has some stuff that should fit you."

Lucas nodded gratefully and bounded up the steps.

While the others took turns using the two downstairs bathrooms, Carla went upstairs and ducked into a half bath, where she discovered she'd bled through. Great. When she explained the situation to Amalia, she rolled her eyes.

"Mother Nature waits for no bitch."

Armed with a small wicker basket filled with pads and tampons, a fresh pair of underwear, and a pair of black joggers, Carla quickly got herself sorted out. She eyed the jacuzzi tub with longing before she pulled the door shut behind her.

Lucas joined them, wearing light-wash jeans, a navy crew neck sweater, and a pained expression. He looked ready to walk the halls of an ivy league college or board a yacht. Eric smirked.

Amalia appeared, holding a rifle and a box of ammunition, which she thrust toward Yuki. Yuki stared at the offering so long, Carla was afraid she'd changed her mind, but then she accepted them with quiet solemnity.

They entered Amalia's home office at the front of the apartment overlooking Ocean View Drive. Beyond it, the skinny, twisting tree-lined streets rose into the San Refugio Hills. To the left, a window looked out over Cortina Creek, rushing toward the lagoon that eventually opened to the ocean. The creek was a log-filled, muddy torrent overflowing its banks.

Yuki removed the rifle's scope and peered through it at the creek-side neighborhood where she had lived with her husband.

Carla swallowed. "Anything out there?"

"The damage is bad farther up the creek," Yuki said, eye still pressed to the scope. She sighed. "The water made it all the way up to our house, but that's not a surprise. It won't be the first time it's flooded. Matt would hate to see this. He spent the whole summer putting in the new deck, and it's a total wreck." She paused. "Oh, oh. My neighbors are on the roof of their house."

Natale squinted at the creek. "Maybe those things got inside."

"It's possible," Yuki said. "With the high tide, water from the ocean washed up the creek. But I hope not. It's a family with two kids."

Natalie clutched the pearl pendant hanging from a chain around her neck and pressed it to her bottom lip. "Are they all right?"

"They're alive."

When Natalie left to join the others across the room, Yuki lowered the scope and turned toward Carla. Desolation had dulled the brightness in her eyes.

Carla lightly tapped Yuki's arm. "Are you okay?"

Yuki sniffed. "My soulmate is dead. I am not okay, but we're going to kill those motherfuckers, and the sooner the better."

Carla's heart fluttered. Yuki wasn't given to swearing, and Carla took it as a sign of hope. A focused, pissed-off Yuki was better than a sad, listless Yuki, especially when it involved blowing things up with that rifle.

She was surprised and slightly offended Yuki had never told her about hitting the shooting range with Axel, but now wasn't the time to ask why she had chosen to keep that secret.

Peter and Lucas had already cleared the furniture in front of the largest window overlooking the street. Amalia said it was twelve feet to the ground. Cold, damp air blew inside. If this part of the plan worked, they'd be outside soon. If it didn't, Lucas could have sprained an ankle, or worse.

Carla's throat tightened as she watched Lucas open the window, then clamber over the sill, a jumble of knees and elbows maneuvering himself into position. His long legs dangled, the toes of his sneakers bumping against the building. Eric grabbed his forearms. To Carla's surprise, Eric had insisted on being the one to help Lucas.

"I lift weights heavier than that guy," he'd said.

Eric bent over the sill, hands locked around Lucas's thin wrists, and slowly began to lower Lucas toward the ground. Peter and Carla held Eric's legs in place as he stretched as far out of the window as he could.

"You got this?" Eric grunted.

Carla squeezed her eyes shut and waited, holding her breath. A moment later, she heard a thud, followed by a yell.

"Lucas!" Eric cried. "You okay?"

A grim laugh drifted up from below. "Yeah, I'm just fucking with you. I'm fine."

Peter released his hold on Eric's legs and stuck his head out the window. "Take that street to the fire truck and bring the longest ladder you can carry."

Carla leaned out and gave Lucas a thumbs-up. His eyes snapped open in surprise. He returned the gesture, a little stiffly. His sweater had hiked up, exposing his flat, brown stomach. He yanked it down and turned his attention back to Peter.

"Aren't the ladders padlocked or something?"

Peter shook his head. "They never bother. Not around here. There are a couple of those grates as you get closer to the bridge, so stay away from those."

"Would you let him go already?" Natalie muttered behind them.

Eric shoved his hands in his pockets, watching Lucas race across the empty street, then disappear around a corner. "That guy is so skinny. Can he even carry a ladder?"

Peter tipped his head back and groaned. "Please. Don't say that."

Carla bristled. "He's wiry, but he's strong."

Chapter 41

light breezes

Carla hugged Lucas when she hopped off the ladder and stared down at her dirty, wet sneakers. Two feet on solid ground had never felt so good.

They could leave. Drive out. Eric had parked his news van up the hill, where it was safe from the water. They could all fit in it, probably.

Those demon fish belonged in the water. They hadn't sprouted legs and charged up Carla's stairs in pursuit. If they stayed out of the monsters' reach, they were safe. Free. Now that they'd managed to escape the crumbling building with its lagoon of monsters, all they had to do was wait for the professionals to arrive. Scientists. The FBI. Whatever secret government agency dealt with aliens and other unexplained phenomenon. It seemed the worst sort of hubris to believe they could kill the creatures themselves.

"We don't have to do this," she said.

Peter turned toward her, eyebrows raised. "What do you mean? I thought we agreed."

"Hey, boomers," Natalie called. "What's going on over there? Anything we should know about?"

"Who the hell is she calling 'boomers'?" Peter muttered.

Carla bristled. She'd adjusted to the notion the young people thought of her and Peter as parental figures, but grandparents? No way. She waved the others over.

"I was just about to say we don't have to try to kill those things ourselves. We're free to go. And what if we're wrong? What if the scientists need those things alive to study them?"

Eric frowned. "I doubt that. Scientists can tell a whole lot by dissecting them."

Lucas snorted. "There won't be anything to dissect, remember? We're going to blow them to bits."

"We hope," Yuki said.

Eric bit his lip, uncertainty written across his face.

"We have to do it," Natalie said hotly. "Now. If we don't, they might swim out, and then good luck trying to catch them."

Amalia nodded. "She's right. Trying to cull them once they're out in the bay would be next to impossible, especially if they're from the deep. They'll just hide down there."

"We're wasting time!" Natalie cried.

"Yeah, we are," Lucas muttered. He dropped his gaze from Carla and shot Peter a pleading look.

Amalia held up her hands. "And, as I was about to say, there's something else. What if there are pregnant females? Don't we want to kill them before they add to their population?"

"Oh, hell no." Carla swallowed. The mere thought was terrifying. Suddenly, leaving without at least trying to kill those creatures seemed irresponsible.

Peter grabbed her hand and gave it a squeeze. "Carla's right. If anyone has second thoughts or wants to do things differently, now's the time to talk about it. But I'm in. All in. We can't afford to wait for help to arrive, and when it finally does, we can't be sure they'll do the right thing."

Peter spoke with conviction. Carla felt a wave of relief wash over her. Whatever crisis of confidence Peter had been dealing with, he seemed to have regained his footing. Suddenly, her idea of leaving San Refugio seemed like a craven dereliction of duty.

"You don't have to ask me twice," Natalie said.

Eric gave a curt nod, chin high. "Me either. I just hope Yuki doesn't screw up this time."

Yuki ignored him and gave the box of ammunition a good shake. "If Matt were here, he'd want us to do this."

"I'm in," Lucas said.

"You already know where I stand," Amalia added. "I am for a culling."

Carla and Peter left the others sitting on upside-down benches clustered in the middle of the street, surrounded by a pile of driftwood and white plastic chairs. Carla suspected the cheap chairs were from the back deck of Bigg's Bar. He had been too frugal to buy something nicer.

She sighed. The man's dead body was still in his apartment, and with what they were planning to do, he'd never have the open casket funeral he'd always joked about.

"I put it in my will for the funeral home to make me up like The Joker. That's a good one, right? That'll give my son something to remember. That's his favorite movie."

The streets were eerily quiet when Carla and Peter crossed the bridge over Cortina Creek.

"I guess everyone evacuated," Peter said.

She paused long enough to peer at the homes lining the creek. The mayor had a place there.

"Except for us. I can't believe they still haven't sent anybody down here."

On her right, homes were wedged between the cliff and the street leading up the hill. A massive new house with lots of glass and white-painted wood loomed over the surf. Modern farmhouse, Yuki had called it on one of their walks. It sat next to a much smaller, older home that hadn't been updated in decades. That was San Refugio. A mix of newcomers with lots of money and people who'd bought years ago—or like Peter, who'd inherited their properties.

On her left, cars and trucks—Peter's included—were bunched together, piled against the back wall of the condos.

"Well, shit." Peter walked over to his truck, sandwiched between an old Honda and a Volkswagen Westfalia. Seaweed covered the tires, and a line of foamy scum along the body showed how high the water had been.

He reached into the bed and unlocked the storage bin.

"Still dry." He held up a black fabric case.

Peter unzipped it and checked the contents, exhaling loudly.

"Twelve left. I've had these things so long, I forgot how many I had."

Peter had explained the propane tanks wouldn't explode by just shooting holes in them. They needed a spark to make that happen. The flares would provide that spark, even if they got wet.

If the flares didn't work, the plan would fail.

Chapter 42

storm surge 0.2 ft

The door to Carla's restaurant appeared wide enough. It wouldn't take much to lob the road flares inside. But tossing flares while staying well out of range of deadly tentacles was a different story.

The mangled bodies of the firefighters lay on the ground. Whoever was going to throw the flares would have to ignore the hideous pile of corpses.

Eric and Lucas argued over who was best suited for the job.

"Playing video games does not mean you have a good arm," Eric snapped.

Lucas snorted dismissively. "Playing baseball in high school doesn't either."

Natalie stepped forward, seething. "This is such patriarchal bullshit. What makes you two think you're the only ones who can throw? Because you have penises?"

Lucas winced and dipped his head. "So…what? Like, you can?"

Natalie pressed her lips together, her gaze shifting to the door. "I'm positive I can."

Peter was only half listening. At the far edges of his mind, a memory stirred, an important one he couldn't quite recall.

"What makes you so sure you can do it?" Eric folded his arms in front of his chest.

"I belong to an axe-throwing club. We meet every Friday night after work. My aim has gotten pretty good."

"That's a real thing?" Lucas asked, voice rising.

Natalie sniffed dismissively. "Yes, it's a real thing. It's a fun way to de-stress." She paused. "Olivia talked me into joining, so if I can use my skills to help kill the things that killed her, you can say I have every motivation in the world."

"Motivation isn't enough," Eric muttered, then shrugged. "But whatever Peter decides."

All eyes turned to Peter. Once again, everyone assumed he was the de facto leader. But the dynamics had changed. Amalia was a sea captain with an impressive set of qualifications. Just because he was a former state lifeguard—and a man—didn't mean he was automatically in charge.

He turned to Amalia. "What do you think?"

"I think we should trust Natalie. We have twelve flares. We could give her three chances, and if she can't manage it, then Lucas and Eric can try their luck." She pointed at Carla. "How about you? Any good at throwing?"

"Not really," Carla said.

Peter's mouth fell open. That was it. The thing he was trying to remember. "Yes, you are. I've seen you. You can hurl a beer can right into the trash from across the room. Every single time."

Yuki smiled weakly. "I forgot about that. But definitely. She can even chuck champagne mini bottles too."

Carla wasn't as enthusiastic as Natalie about the role of flare thrower, but she agreed, warily eyeing the door, expecting something to come out of it at any moment.

Peter wondered why they hadn't seen the creatures since they climbed out of the building. Probably because no one had gotten close enough. Or maybe the things had escaped back into the bay, and they'd missed their opportunity. Since Amalia mentioned the likelihood of pregnant females, a knot of dread had formed in his stomach and remained coiled there.

Yuki searched for a spot that provided good visibility into the restaurant. "That'll do it," she said, pointing at an overhang above Bruno's BBQ, the bright red restaurant directly across the street from Carla's.

She hurried toward a large tree trunk that had been swept in by the tide and was lodged against the building. Handing Peter the rifle, she clambered up the trunk and onto the wooden overhang.

Peter had to stretch to pass the rifle to Yuki. She looked down at him with a weary smile. "When they remodeled this place, I hated it. So cheesy, right? And who wants to eat messy barbeque at the beach? But remind me to thank the Brunos when I see them again."

Peter watched her gather her long hair and tie it up into a tight bun. Yuki lowered herself to a kneeling position and pressed her eye against the scope.

"I can see six tanks."

"Do you see…them?" *Them.* Privately, Peter thought of them as *creatures.* Or *monsters,* but he hadn't found the right word to say out loud.

"No. If they're there, they're pretty good at hiding."

"Do you need anything else from me?" He cleared his throat. "Should we go through it again?"

Yuki lowered the rifle and inhaled through her nose, then exhaled loudly. "You're going to light the flares. Carla and Natalie will try to get them as close as possible to the tanks. I'll shoot the tanks, and that should get things started."

Peter wiped his forehead. He felt sweaty despite the chilly morning air. "That's it."

When he turned around, Carla was doing side lunges, clasping a flare as though it were a dumbbell. Natalie had her eyes trained on the entrance, moving around, testing stances, braids hanging down her back.

Peter pointed at a log resting about a dozen feet from the lifeless bodies of the three firefighters. "Don't go beyond that point."

He didn't know how long the tentacles stretched out, and he could only hope the enormous creature they had seen at the end of the dock hadn't made its way into the restaurant.

A siren sounded in the distance.

Carla's head jerked toward the noise. Natalie froze, mouth open.

"Let's go!" Peter yanked on the tab of the first flare, revealing a brown cap. Directing the flare away from himself and his two companions, he peeled away the waxy red paper, twisted off the cap, and used it to strike the black disc at the top of the flare.

Nothing. Not a single spark.

Natalie groaned. "Are you kidding me?"

Peter was unfazed. The instructions printed on the side of the flare never worked for him, and he'd come prepared. He reached into his pocket and produced a lighter he kept in the kit.

The flare burst to life, an orange crackling flame shooting a stream of sparks into the air. Natalie snatched it from his hand, marched up to the log in the street, and flung it away. The flare sparked through the air until it struck the side of the building. It fell to the ground, bounced a few times, and came to rest, still sizzling, a foot away from Jones's outstretched hand.

"Shit!" Natalie paced in a tight circle, hands pressed against the side of her head.

Peter handed a lit torch to Carla, who took it with grave solemnity. She stepped up to, then past, the safety line and lobbed the flare inside. Attention still fixed on the door, she reached back over her shoulder and snapped her fingers.

Peter hastily lit another flare. Ignoring Natalie's reproachful stare, he passed it to Carla, who launched it into the flooded restaurant. Within seconds, a third flare followed and then a fourth. From afar, Lucas cheered.

"They're all where they should be," Yuki cried, voice triumphant.

There were only seven left. Each critical.

Natalie stepped forward and extended her hand. "Please. Let me try again."

Carla hovered behind her, expression unreadable. She gave an almost imperceptible shrug.

The siren continued to blare in the distance, but it wasn't getting any closer. Maybe due to a downed tree, or maybe they were headed to another emergency.

Peter lit another flare and handed it to Natalie. Biting her lip, she snatched it from his hand and ran up to the line. From the set of her shoulders, Peter could imagine the look of fierce concentration on her face. With a swift motion, she hurled the flare inside.

"She did it," Yuki shouted.

Natalie pumped her fists into the air and spun around, grinning.

Peter watched Yuki raise the rifle and take aim. He heard the crack of the rifle, followed by a sharp metallic clang and a hissing sound when the bullet hit the tanks. Peter couldn't see what was going on inside, but he could easily imagine it.

The pressurized propane stored in the tanks would shoot out of the holes at high speed, propelling the tanks backward in a chaotic scene filled with noise, slamming into walls and hard objects bobbing in the flooded restaurant.

And then, suddenly, flames filled the dark space.

Yuki continued shooting, and more tanks began spinning through the water, spewing flame.

Peter stared at the inferno. From the door to Pancha's, a flaming tentacle uncurled, rolling out past the dead firemen. It twitched as if trying to find its prey, then collapsed onto the sidewalk, the flames consuming the black stalk.

Behind Peter, Lucas and Natalie cheered.

The plan was working, but still Peter felt numb, unable to join the victorious howls.

He had no way of knowing if the flames had taken out all of them. If some of the things had taken refuge at the bottom of the flooded restaurant, the thick layer of debris might have protected them from the pandemonium above. All they needed to do was wait until the flames went out.

And what if there were hundreds more in the bay?

Peter could feel his optimism fading. The plan seemed almost silly now—the concoction of children playing at saving the Monterey Bay from creatures that had tormented them through the night. He felt like a fool for thinking it would actually work. How could he have been so naive?

Peter turned away from the scene.

By Carla's crestfallen expression, she was having similar thoughts. With a sigh, his back to Pancha's Restaurant, he pulled Carla close and squeezed his eyes shut.

Even if they hadn't killed all the creatures, at least they were safe, he reminded himself. They'd escaped the building and were now out of harm's way.

The ground trembled beneath him, and a deafening roar exploded behind them.

Peter could feel a sudden rush of air and heat on his back. Shards of glass and debris rained down from the sky. Yuki was already on the ground. Carla pulled him under the overhang to escape the falling detritus. Spinning around, he saw a cloud of smoke and flame.

"Oh my God, what happened?" Natalie cried.

Peter scanned the scene. Pancha's Restaurant was obliterated, reduced to a smoldering pile of rubble. So were Bigg's Bar and Harmon's Restaurant. With the buildings gone, he could see the gray ocean and the waves still crashing onto the beach.

At the far left end, the vacation rental slowly collapsed onto its pilings.

The propane tanks, even with flares burning around them, couldn't have done all that.

And then he remembered.

"The gas leak," he said, then began to laugh.

Chapter 43

thin high clouds

The storm had retreated, leaving behind a sullen gray sky and a trail of devastation in San Refugio. While most of the damage happened in the hills where the trees were thickest, what happened along the curve of beach between the pier and the bandshell shocked public officials and the community.

Power was back on in most places, and mobile service had been restored. But the majority of the village of San Refugio was off limits while officials picked through the rubble and cleared the debris on the roads. Peter's condo was behind yellow caution tape, and he'd be unable to return home until officials gave the all-clear.

The operator of the drone had posted a teaser clip on social media. After a bidding frenzy from some less-than-reputable media outlets, he had sold the video footage to the radio talk show host who had also bought Ken Bigg's photo of the creature he'd captured.

From their temporary home—a vacation rental that slept eight people—Peter listened to the radio host rant and rave about monsters and conspiracies, waiting for his coffee to brew and staring out at the bay. There was plenty of action out there. Lots more boats than usual—the largest belonging to the marine science lab leading the search for the sea creatures.

Peter was now convinced his neighbor Maggie had fallen victim to those things, and he told Sheriff Ackerman where to find her body. The only intact victim. There wasn't much left of the dead firefighters on Ocean View Drive.

231

A multi-agency effort to search the water beneath Carla's restaurant was probably underway. The sheriff said they weren't taking any chances and were sending in remote operated vehicles equipped with sonar and cameras to inspect the area.

Peter hadn't held anything back when describing their terrifying night during his interview with the sheriff, and neither had anyone else in their sad little group of survivors. They hadn't used words like "monster" or "creature" to describe the things in the water. It wasn't necessary. All they needed to do was describe them and leave it to the sheriff to form his own conclusions.

Before Eric left for the TV station, he said his mother and the other scientists would want to interview them too. And sure enough, Peter had awakened to a message from Jessica Chen, asking if she could stop by as soon as she could get there. While she was interested in talking to anyone who was available, it was Carla with whom she seemed most eager to speak.

Peter heard pipes clanking and groaning. On the second floor, someone was showering.

When he poured his second cup of coffee, a helicopter flew low along the length of San Refugio Beach. The radio talk show host was going on about Ken Bigg's theory: lab-created human-fish hybrids had escaped from a top-secret government facility.

Peter was about to switch to another station when the host referred to a bit of news he'd somehow managed to miss, one involving the tentacled creature they'd seen at the end of the pier.

"So, what is the truth behind this video, folks? The officials now say it's an AI-generated image. In case you've been living under a rock,

AI stands for artificial intelligence, and that means we're supposed to believe the video is fake. But I'm not buying it, and neither should you because that's a government cover-up for something far more sinister. Something they don't want us regular, hardworking Americans to know about because the elites in some fancy government-sponsored laboratory got up to the Devil's work. Now whether those things escaped or someone let them out intentionally is something we may never know, but I'll remind you that two days ago, two men were killed by a mysterious thing in the waters of the Monterey Bay, and then after a catastrophic storm, a creature with tentacles rises out of the water. Do not trust this 'official explanation,' folks. Connect the dots. Pull the threads. Contact your local representative and start getting the answers you deserve.

"And whatever you do, stay away from the beach."

Peter couldn't abide the talk show host and his theories, but he couldn't shake the feeling there might be some truth to what he was saying. He'd seen the creature in the video. Peter knew it was real. And now somebody didn't want the truth to get out. What better way to do that than claim it was the work of AI?

He groaned. Thinking it was one thing. Saying it aloud would make him sound as crazy as Ken. The poor bastard. He guessed it was up to the sheriff's office to contact his son in Texas. The same went for Maggie. She had a daughter around his age in Sacramento who worked as a nurse. Whatever the coroner might have to say about her mother's death, she was sure to have questions.

Peter washed his mug in the sink. The chopper was gone. Another large boat had arrived—modern lines, painted blue and white.

It was odd being able to see the water and not hear it. But after what he'd just experienced, he found it restful. The roaring surf had brought worry, anxiety, and then terror.

The vacation rental on the bluff belonged to an old friend who'd retired to Sedona, preferring the red rock desert to the central coast. Like Peter's condo, it needed updating, so while the view was spectacular, it didn't fare so well in the tourist rental market. But Peter liked it. The rooms were big, the furniture old-fashioned but comfortable. And he loved the solid wood casement windows that opened out when you turned the crank.

His friend had offered to sell him the place, but he'd never seriously considered it. Maybe he should. Peter still hadn't been allowed back into his flooded disaster of a condo. He could hire one of those water damage restoration companies, but that would cost a fortune, and now that he was retired, there was no reason not to do the work himself. It was sure to be a tiring, miserable business.

His phone chimed.

A message from Jessica Chen. Could she come by now? Was Carla available?

The kitchen door swung open. Carla walked through, hair wet and tied back in a ponytail, wearing clothes she'd borrowed from Amalia. Black joggers and a loose cream-colored sweater.

He crossed the room and took her in his arms. She leaned against him, limp. Her hair smelled of musk and citrus. He'd seen the fancy shampoo bottle in the bathroom, another of Amalia's offerings before she'd left for the night.

Her eyes moved to the window. "What's going on?"

"A lot. It looks like there's a search going on, but at the same time, the official word is, the drone footage is a fake made by AI. And Eric's mom is on her way over because she wants to talk to you."

Carla pulled away, frowning. "Me?"

234

Peter didn't know why Jessica Chen was so interested in talking to Carla, but icy fingers of dread traced the length of his spine.

Chapter 44

57°

The adrenaline was gone from her body. Carla felt empty, strangely flat, like a cardboard cutout. And yet, a flicker of curiosity broke through her daze as she watched Jessica Chen lower herself into the chair opposite. Peter sat next to Carla on a lumpy loveseat, and by the way he gripped her hand, she wondered if he knew more about the purpose of the scientist's visit than he'd admitted.

Jessica perched at the edge of her chair, crossing and uncrossing her legs, clearing her throat.

It was early. Not even eight o'clock. Lucas and Natalie were still sleeping upstairs. She had decided to stay to meet Olivia's parents, who were driving up from Los Angeles, to explain, as best she could, what had happened to their daughter.

Carla guessed it would be some time before Yuki awoke. Unable to relax, she'd prowled the house until the early hours of the morning and had fallen asleep just after sunrise. Amalia and Eric were the only two in their group who had refused Peter's offer to stay at the rambling house on the bluff.

Jessica looked more like Eric's older sister than his mother, wearing jeans and a flannel shirt, her dark hair in a short, wispy cut.

She bit her lip and then took a deep breath. "I'm so sorry to bring this up after everything you've been through. Eric told me all of it. And I just want you to know that I believe it. He sent me a copy of his video yesterday, and I've spent all night looking at it…"

Peter interrupted. "It wasn't on the morning news."

"No," Jessica replied briskly. "The company that owns the station wouldn't let them run it. It's being authenticated. They're suspicious it might be a fake."

"It's not," Carla said.

"I know." Jessica shrugged. "Eric wouldn't do that. But I know it's real, and so do the people I work with." She hesitated, the beginnings of a rueful smile playing around her lips. "They finally believe me. Eric said he told you what I saw in the water a few years ago. That's why I'm here. That's why I wanted to talk to you." She leaned forward, staring directly at Carla. "I'm sorry I have to do this. I don't want to upset you."

Jessica's tone remained crisp and businesslike, but it wasn't enough to disguise the scientist's restless unease.

Suddenly, Carla wanted nothing more than to run from the room. Go back to bed and pull the comforter over her head. Instead, she got up and crossed to the window. From the angle high on the bluff, she couldn't see Ocean View Drive or the charred and flattened remains of her restaurant. Cortina Creek was still swollen with muddy water, the surf around the storm-wrecked pier a brownish gray.

She was buying time. To think. To prepare herself for whatever this stranger had to say. Her mind refused to settle. When she turned to face Jessica, the scientist was rocking slightly in her chair, knees pressed together.

Carla could feel Peter's gaze but avoided looking at him. "All right," she said loudly. "Whatever it is, just say it."

Jessica's chin jutted out. "I'd like to ask if you'd be willing to give me a DNA sample."

Whatever Carla had been expecting, it wasn't that. "Why?"

"I understand your son was among the group of people who died in that terrible boating accident in the middle of the bay a few years ago. I'll be asking all the families to contribute DNA samples as…" Jessica began to stammer. "As…the bodies were never recovered."

Carla sat on the loveseat next to Peter and stared at the woman, the shadow of suspicion darkening the edges of her mind. "Why do you need our DNA?"

"To determine if there's any connection to the DNA we've taken from the wounds of the men attacked yesterday. There was a woman too. I understand they collected her body last night."

Peter was shaking his head. "That was my neighbor, Maggie. I found her. I didn't see any obvious wounds."

"It was at the base of her spine," Jessica said.

Peter squeezed his eyes shut and flopped back against the couch. "Jesus. I missed it."

Carla didn't hear any of that. Her mind was racing, generating possibilities, each more horrifying than the last. "But why would you think there's any connection between my son and those people? What the hell are you trying to say?"

"It's just a theory at this point," Jessica replied, staring down at her hands. "But the venom we've analyzed contains some human DNA…"

Carla felt her throat seize, as if an invisible hand were choking off her air supply. She gasped. "Wait. Are you saying you think those things have something to do with my son?"

"They might, yes." Jessica gave a curt nod.

Peter shifted next to her. Carla felt his arm go around her shoulder and pull her close.

"Are you fucking kidding me?"

"No. Of course not." Jessica's voice was low but steady. "I know this is a shock, but I'd like to explain. If you'll let me."

Carla felt like the floor had opened, swallowing her in a fathomless black hole.

Chapter 45

humidity 43%

Carla listened to Jessica Chen in horrified silence. She wanted to run screaming, clap her hands over her ears like a child, yell "shut up, shut up, shut up" until the woman stopped spewing nonsense.

The world no longer made sense. But Jessica kept on, assaulting Carla's sense of reality. Every new bit of information followed by, "…but we don't know for sure."

Somehow, through some inexplicable process of nature, Jessica Chen thought it was possible that a part of Jacob lived on.

Carla knew Jessica had seen a humanoid shape swimming in the depths of the Monterey Bay because her son, Eric, had told them. But he'd omitted a critical part. The part that explained what the robotic craft was doing in that spot. It wasn't in some random location.

The remote-operated submersible had been lowered to the canyon floor, where the shipwreck lurked, to map its location and take samples of the water and wildlife.

The mission had ended in catastrophe. The submersible had malfunctioned and imploded. But not before collecting samples and transmitting a stream of data. Some of it was noteworthy and surprising. It showed elevated water temperatures and evidence of a new virus affecting deep sea creatures living near hydrothermal vents on the floor of the bay.

Jessica's theory sent an electric ripple up Carla's spine. Her hands tingled.

She said fish and cephalopods infected with this virus might have come into contact with the victims of the shipwreck.

"We think there may have been some horizontal gene transfer. It's something we're looking into."

There was a cough at the door. It was Lucas, dark hair mussed.

"I thought that only happened in plants?" From his expression, he'd been standing there long enough to hear Jessica's explanation.

Jessica glanced at him in surprise. Carla knew that look. Not long ago, she'd also underestimated Lucas.

"It's happened in fish too," Jessica said.

Lucas paled. "But still. What you're saying is pretty wild."

"It is." Jessica gave a curt nod. "And just to be clear, it's still a theory. Not all my colleagues agree. Some believe the things you encountered—and even the large one documented by the drone—are new to the bay. In fact, mine is a minority opinion, but the powers that be are giving me the opportunity to pursue it." There was a bitter edge to her voice. "It would help if we had a body to study."

Peter rose and began pacing around the room. Carla's stomach rolled. She swallowed.

"Before Ken Bigg died—the guy who owned the bar next to me—he was talking about hybrids. Is that what these things are? Were? Some sort of cross between a human and a fish?"

Still hovering at the door, Lucas coughed again. Carla waved him over and pointed at the vacant chair next to Jessica. He'd earned the right to be a part of the conversation.

In the soft morning light, his complexion had taken on a pale cast.

"They're not really hybrids, are they?" Lucas asked. He gripped the arms of the chair as if it were about to take off.

Jessica's mouth opened, then closed. She rubbed her throat before she replied. "No. Not in the sense you're talking about." She paused. "That would be…impossible."

Carla stiffened. She'd managed to follow Jessica's explanation despite all the technical terms. Now, Jessica and Lucas seemed to be having a private conversation, one she didn't understand. Something at the edges of her consciousness nagged at her, trying to make itself heard, but her thinking had gone fuzzy.

She glanced at Peter, who was leaning against a wall next to a vintage surfboard hanging from a set of decorative hooks. He was frowning, arms crossed in front of his chest.

"What's this about?" Carla asked. Her voice sounded unusually high and thin to her own ears.

The uneasy glance between Jessica and Lucas did not escape her.

"Well?"

Jessica scraped a hand through her hair. "When people talk about hybrids, it means crossbreeding through normal sexual processes. That's not what we're talking about here because…" Her voice drifted off. After a moment, she pushed back her shoulders and sat a little straighter. "Because that's not possible here, Carla. Your son and the others drowned, and even if they hadn't, crossbreeding between species is impossible."

There was a roaring in Carla's ears. The words wouldn't form, so she nodded instead. She pushed the idea away, then slammed the door behind it.

Peter cleared his throat. "One of them seemed to have human features. It could also unhinge its jaw."

"I can't account for that. It could have just been coincidence. Some fish have surprising adaptations that make them look like they have human-like features. But what I think is that human genes transferred to the fish, thanks to a parasitic vector, the virus. The result is a new species."

"Jesus," Peter said. "After what we saw, I actually believe it."

Carla pressed a hand against her chest and tried to regain control of her breathing. "There's one thing I don't understand. If they're part human, why would they try to kill us?"

Jessica didn't look happy with the question. "I don't know. Maybe their predator instincts were strong. Maybe the virus made them sick, and it caused behavioral abnormalities." She hesitated. "The other thing we don't know is why they came ashore. We think the storm had something to do with it. Maybe it disoriented them. We think they're from the deep sea, so maybe they got the bends coming rapidly to the surface and that affected their brains. But I have to ask. Lucas counted eleven of them in your restaurant. That's a lot in that space, confined as it was. And from what you said, they could have left at any time. Is there any reason you can think of why they would have gathered at your place?"

She knew the answer. But to say the words meant to suggest something nobody had mentioned. Yet. It meant there was much more going on than simply a combination of genes. And it meant that, in a way, the people who died that day on the water lived on in some form.

Carla fought back tears. "Jacob told everyone to meet at the restaurant for breakfast before they left that morning. It's the last place they all were before the accident."

It was horrible and tragic and impossible—that those creatures had vague memories of the crew's and students' final hours on land and had sought out her place as a refuge from the storm. That those creatures were made up of remnants of the people who died. She shuddered, trying to push the idea out of her mind.

Everyone sat quietly as Carla wiped the tears from her eyes and worked to regain her composure. Jessica quietly made notes. Lucas stared at the floor. Peter stood behind Carla and put his hands on her shoulders.

They stayed like that for a long time, Carla thinking about what might have brought the sea creatures to Pancha's Restaurant. About what it might mean if the creatures had fragments of human memory.

After a couple of minutes, Lucas leaned forward. "Can I ask a question, Dr. Chen?"

She gave him a tired smile. "Of course."

"I'm confused by something. Olivia's body seemed to be changing. It was going all gray and shiny. It looked like she was turning into something else. A fish. Eric thought so too. That's why he wanted to throw Olivia back into the water. Just in case she was…infectious. So, you think that's not what was happening?"

Jessica seemed relieved to be talking once again about science. She shook her head. "No, I don't think that's what's happening. That's not how horizontal gene transfer works. The effect isn't immediate. The genes have to make it into the cells of the other species, then the fish need to reproduce. I believe these creatures were the offspring of those original fish that came into contact with humans. I suspect what you were seeing were just the effects of the venom."

Carla glanced nervously at the door to make sure Yuki wasn't there. She wasn't, but Carla lowered her voice anyway. "What about Matt and the other man who was stung? What happened to them? Did their bodies continue to change after they were put in freezers or wherever?"

Jessica got to her feet. "That's a very good question and one I can actually answer with confidence. I talked with the hospital on my drive over. The bodies are discolored due to the venom. That's all. But it is under investigation." Grabbing her blue canvas tote bag from the floor, she rummaged inside and pulled out a small metallic pouch. Her expression softened. "I need to go, but I'd like to get that DNA sample from you. If you're still willing."

Carla nodded, feeling numb.

If the test proved a link between her son and those terrifying creatures, it was something she'd have to grapple with for the rest of her life.

Chapter 46

light westerly breeze

After Jessica Chen left, Carla went outside and stared at the ocean for a long time. Then, without a word, she went into the bedroom and quietly pulled the door shut behind her. When Peter peeked in an hour later, Carla was asleep, the comforter pulled up over her head.

When she finally emerged, Peter could tell something had changed. Carla inventoried the kitchen, made a grocery list, then together, they drove through the storm-damaged streets of San Refugio to a grocery store.

"FEMA's going to set up an office in the village so business owners can apply for disaster assistance," she said.

Peter didn't dare take his eyes off the road. He steered his smelly, battered truck through an obstacle course of downed tree limbs, drooping power lines, and pools of water. And his head still hurt from hitting the booze too hard the night before. "How do you know?"

She tapped her phone resting in the center console. Cell service had been restored. "The city manager. He's been keeping us up to date. I have a lot of catching up to do." Carla paused. "They put out a press release saying the firefighters were killed in the gas explosion. The mayor is asking us not to make any public comments about the drone video or all the research ships hanging around just offshore."

"Have you said anything to anyone? About what we saw?"

"No. And I don't plan to, unless Eric does his news story and shows the video. People already think I'm a little off after

Jacob died. That would really do it. I'd be known as the crazy lady who snapped during the storm. How about you? People would believe you."

Peter could feel her staring at him. A bitter laugh escaped his throat. "No, they wouldn't. You saw what happened when I tried to warn Jones. He blew me off. That's what everyone will do if I start talking about monsters in the water. Jesus, Carla. What if there's a whole bunch of them out there and they can't be caught or killed? That's what we're not talking about. What if the water is infested with them?" His voice was loud and angry.

Carla squeezed his leg. "We talked about it plenty last night after you and Lucas killed that bottle of scotch, and it solved nothing. If those things come back, they'll ruin beach life as we know it. Here and up and down the coast. All we can do is hope Jessica Chen can get some support so scientists and the government can come up with a plan."

"You make it sound like the apocalypse." The hair lifted on the back of his neck.

Inside the grocery store, it was business as usual. The lights were on. The shelves were fully stocked. There was even a line at the butcher counter. People were talking about the storm but only how it affected their property and neighborhoods.

It was both reassuring and disturbing.

Peter was glad to be in a place where people were talking about normal problems, like trees crushing cars and sheds, but also worried about the disconnect it revealed. Not many people lived close enough to the beach to be directly impacted by the appearance of strange, deadly creatures. If there was a problem at the beach, they could simply avoid it. Unless the problem migrated to the other shores. Then there would be a public outcry about falling property values and tourism drying up, but by then, it would be too late.

Peter was so distracted by these dark, spiraling thoughts that he wasn't paying attention to where he was steering the grocery cart and bumped it into a woman's plump backside.

She whirled around and glared at him. "I hope you don't drive your car like that."

He muttered his profuse apologies, then pushed the cart around the corner to escape the woman's hostile stare.

Carla appeared a few moments later, smirking. "Can't take you anywhere."

On the drive home, they tried to find a radio news program talking about San Refugio Beach. Mostly, the few stories they managed to catch focused on the devastating damage caused by the storm surge and the impact of climate change on low-lying coastal communities. The local public radio station did a story about the rise of deepfake scams, using the video of the enormous tentacles on San Refugio Pier as the primary example. An expert from a local college said she'd run the image through several programs designed to catch AI-generated images and came to a different conclusion than had the officials. She thought the image was real.

That angle went nowhere fast. Another expert from a prestigious university disagreed. The video was not only fake, but probably had been inspired by fatal venomous stings from an unidentified cartilaginous fish that had happened the day before.

To Peter, all that seemed like a hundred years ago.

And then the voice of the mayor of San Refugio came on, complaining about the terrible rumors circulating on social media and through irresponsible talk show hosts, describing human-fish hybrids. If that wasn't the most ridiculous thing she had ever heard. When asked about the number of marine scientists who descended on the town, she didn't hesitate.

"We've had two fatalities involving some kind of stingray that's not native to our area, so I for one am glad to have all the expert help we can get to make sure our waters remain safe for the public."

Carla slapped the dashboard. "So much for not giving interviews. She never could keep her mouth shut." Carla fumed all the way to San Refugio.

When they crested the hill, they could see activity on the beach. Peter squinted into the fading light, trying to figure out what was happening. Beside him, Carla sat up straight, straining against her seatbelt.

There was something on the sand, the water crashing over it. Something big and dark. They were still too far away to tell what was happening.

And then he remembered. "There are binoculars in the glove compartment."

When Carla couldn't figure out how to adjust them quickly enough to suit him, Peter pulled over, slammed the truck into park, and hopped out. The wind tugged at his clothes as he stared through the eyepiece.

He could see it. The whole damn thing. A greenish-black blob on the driftwood-littered beach, half hidden by a pile of seaweed, its tentacles spread along the sand as if it was trying to haul itself up the beach.

The same creature they'd seen at the end of the pier.

Chapter 47

53°

They snaked down the twisting road toward the beach but were stopped by uniformed officers standing behind a barricade. Peter parked on a side street halfway up the bluff, and they walked down but were turned back again, that time, a little more sternly.

"We need to go home," Carla said. She'd promised to make dinner for everyone. Suddenly, that was more important than anything. The one thing she *could* control.

Peter's hand froze on the passenger door handle. "Home."

She jerked her head in the general direction of the beach. "As much as we're dying to know what's going on down there, they're not going to let us anywhere near it."

Peter shoved the binoculars back into the glove compartment and took her hands in his. "We don't have to live down there."

Her heart beat a little faster, and she gazed up at his hazel eyes. "I can't anymore. I mean, even after I rebuild, I just can't. Too many bad things happened there. But you've got a prime piece of real estate you need to start thinking about cleaning up soon."

Peter cleared his throat. "Yeah. About that. I've made a decision. While you were napping. I'm going to fix up the condo a bit and sell it once the repairs are done and the complex is back to normal. There's always some rich sucker from Silicon Valley who'll pay top dollar for a place close to the water. But I'm done."

"You're kidding?"

Carla couldn't believe it. Peter loved his condo. She never thought he'd move.

"I'm not kidding," Peter said firmly. He raised one of her hands to his lips and kissed it. "I'm getting too old to deal with this bullshit, and these storm cycles are just going to keep happening. And probably worsening. I'm better off selling while the property values are still high."

"But where will you go?"

"*We*. We can stay right where we are. On the bluff. My buddy's been after me to buy it for years, so while you were sleeping, I called him up. Until the deal goes through, he'll rent it to me."

He pulled away, biting his lip.

"Oh shit. I should have checked with you first. Man. Talk about being a self-centered bachelor. I didn't even think to get your input." Peter dipped his head. "I guess I thought I'd surprise you."

Peter looked so sheepish, Carla laughed.

"You did. But in a good way. And I love the house. It's so comfortable, and it's…"

"…got great views a safe distance from the water," he finished.

Carla smiled grimly, determined not to go down the rabbit hole of grief and despair, thinking of Jacob. "As soon as I get the insurance money, I should be able to contribute. To the house."

Her face suddenly felt like it was on fire. He'd asked her to move in with him, not combine their finances.

Now it was his turn to laugh.

"Wow. I goofed that up too. Let me try that again. Why don't we do the thing? You know. Get married. If you don't mind hitching up with a decrepit retiree. But I'll be working on that. The decrepit part. Yuki's been trying to talk me into doing yoga, and I'm going to give it a try."

Carla turned to look back at the beach. It would be dark soon. People had formed a circle around the creature, close enough that she knew it had to be dead.

After her first marriage crashed and burned, after her only son died, she had thought her chances at ever being happy again were slim. Until Peter walked into her restaurant and she felt the faint flicker of desire, then a true connection with another man. A good man who wasn't put off by her bouts of grief, her occasional crankiness, her abrupt ways. But if Peter was willing to try yoga to improve his body, she could work on the less desirable aspects of her personality.

Carla gave him a quick kiss, then a playful shove toward the truck. "The answer is yes. But we can get all sappy about it later. I've got a dinner to make, and we need to figure out how to get down to the beach to see that fucking thing."

Debra Castaneda

Chapter 48

light breeze

Everyone was sitting around the big table in the huge kitchen. Even Eric was there. He'd shown up after his shift at the TV station, looking dejected. Lucas handed him a beer from the refrigerator, and Natalie peppered him with questions.

Carla listened, slicing skirt steak for carne asada.

"The owners won't let us run the video," Eric began. "They said they won't be able to prove that it's real, and with everyone saying the drone footage was a deepfake, they're freaking out. But I know what's really going on. My news director was in meetings all day with the general manager and the head of sales. I think they deep-sixed it because they're afraid if people see the video, they'll stay away from the beach. Our coverage area is all along the Monterey Bay, and there are a lot of businesses next to the water that buy ad time on our station. They're afraid the video will kill all those local businesses, and without them, we can't survive."

Carla turned around just in time to see Lucas punch Eric in the arm. "Fuck 'em."

Eric's face relaxed into a smile. "Yeah. Fuck 'em."

Lucas fell back into his seat, resting his feet on a rung of Eric's chair. "On the other hand, I kind of agree. I'm one of the people who work at the beach, and I need a job." He groaned. "And a place to live now that my apartment is gone."

Carla froze. With everything happening, she hadn't given any thought to Lucas, who'd just lost his job and his cheap apartment, made possible by Ken Bigg's generosity. Student housing was notoriously expensive in Santa Cruz, and returning home to Salinas would mean driving some eighty miles a day.

And then Peter was standing next to her, his warm breath in her ear. "He could stay here. There's an art studio in the backyard we could fix up, so he'd have some privacy."

She nodded, then turned quickly back to the counter to hide the tears threatening to come. While Peter extended their offer, she chopped cilantro and stirred the thin salsa roja simmering on the stove.

"Are you sure?" Lucas was standing right behind her.

She put down the wooden spoon with a sigh and gave him a quick hug. "Yes, I'm sure. Do you think we'd throw you out on the street? And I'll be opening another restaurant when I can find a spot. The village has always had a Pancha's."

Yuki walked into the kitchen. She'd spent the entire day shut up in her bedroom. When Carla had gone to check on her earlier, she'd heard her friend crying through the door, so she left her alone. Yuki's eyes were still red, but she was freshly showered and alert.

"Bruno's BBQ is closing. The owner texted asking if I'd be interested in taking over their lease." She paused. "Maybe we can open up something together."

Natalie snapped her fingers. "That would be so good. Maybe you could do a modern food court. You can share the same kitchen, but people order from different menus and different counters, and they can sit wherever they like."

"That would totally work," Eric said. "I've been to one of those food halls, and they're great. Maybe you could even find another restaurant to come in with you."

Carla blinked, taken aback. She'd never considered going into business with anyone else. But joining with Yuki made sense. They could split the expense of the lease, cutting down on overhead. And Yuki knew how to decorate. Carla's design skills were sadly lacking.

Yuki was staring at her, hands pressing together.

"That would be great," Carla finally said. When Yuki's disappointed look registered, she quickly added. "Really. I mean it. That would be fantastic, if you think you could stand me."

Yuki sniffed, shot her a thumbs-up, and accepted a cocktail from Peter, who was mixing drinks at the opposite end of the counter.

The kitchen was outdated, but it had plenty of workspace. The entire house had high ceilings and beautiful wood windows. Carla couldn't believe she was going to live there. With Peter. They hadn't even made it official yet, and already, the place felt like home.

When they'd finished dinner, she was feeling more than just a little buzzed from two Manhattans. She glanced out the window. It was dark outside. She went into the living room, dragged a dusty telescope from a corner, and carried it through the French doors to the patio. It took some fiddling before she could see the beach.

The creature was now hidden behind a white tent. It was further up the beach, so it had probably been moved so the tide wouldn't reclaim it. There was no one around. Lights blazed from the large ship anchored off the beach. That's where the scientists had gone for the night, then. Maybe they had decided to wait until they could figure out how to transport it to their lab. Or maybe they didn't want to move it until they gathered more evidence.

Whatever. They needed to get down there fast.

"But how?" Peter asked. "The streets are blocked off. There's no way they're letting anyone down there. You can bet those cops are still there."

She shook her head. "We'll go down the cliff to the bandshell. It's clear. I checked."

Eric was out the door, headed to the news van parked in the driveway. He was gone so long, Carla feared he'd driven back to the station, but he returned minutes later, wearing his backpack. "Let's do this," he said excitedly.

Natalie moved in front of the French doors, hands on her hips. "Do what, exactly? I can't believe you want to go anywhere near that fucking thing. What if it's not dead?"

"Of course, it's dead!" Eric rolled his eyes. "They wouldn't leave it out there like that if it weren't. And it's pretty obvious why we need to go. We need proof these things aren't fake."

Natalie threw her hands in the air. "The scientists are down there! They've seen it. They're dealing with it. That's all the proof the world needs."

Eric inhaled through his nose and exhaled loudly. "I texted my mom. She's staying on that ship. She says most everybody is in for the night, but they're taking turns keeping watch on the carcass. Her shift is starting in a few minutes, so she'll be there when we are. She'll look the other way as long as we don't touch it."

Natalie's eyes widened. "Why would she do that?"

Carla was tired of hearing the two argue. She stepped between them. "Because Jessica probably wants a little insurance." She turned to Eric. "Am I right?"

"That's exactly it."

Natalie shook her head. "But what can we do? They'll just say anything we do is a fake too."

"I have an idea," Carla said. "But everybody needs to bring their phones."

Since Lucas had lost his in Carla's flooded restaurant, Eric loaned him a pink instant camera he used at parties.

The cliff was steep, but someone had cut steps into the hillside, so the climb down was easy enough with flashlights. The wind had picked up, and the night air was chilly.

Within minutes, they were standing in the bandshell, looking out at the ruins of the building where Carla had once lived and worked. Yuki stared, a hand pressed against her mouth. She turned away and hurried toward the sand, long dark hair escaping its braid and whipping around her head.

The white tent loomed on the dark beach. It was enormous.

They knew the creature was dead, but they approached warily. Peter was gripping Carla's hand so hard her fingers hurt. She wriggled free and shook out her hand. He shot her an apologetic look.

Before they could stop him, Eric crawled through a gap at the rear of the tent. A moment later, a flashlight winked on, a bobbing circle of white.

"Holy shit," he said.

Carla slid under the opening and recoiled. Up close, the creature wasn't at all what she expected—an oversized octopus, or maybe a squid. It had greenish-black tentacles, but its head was long and stretched out, thinning toward the bottom, suggesting a neck and the beginnings of a chest. The color was different there too. Lighter. Its large protruding eyes were open. Dead, black, and unseeing. Eyes that were disturbingly human. But the most horrifying part was the way the creature split just below its strange torso, tentacles forming on either side, revealing a dirty white circle of a hard, fibrous substance ringed with lumps that appeared to be teeth. At its center was a black beak, open. It looked strong and sharp enough to rip apart anything that fell into it.

Natalie had her hand clapped over her mouth like she was about to throw up. "Can we do whatever we're supposed to do and get out of here? That thing stinks."

And it did. Carla had been so focused on looking at the animal, the stench hadn't registered. It stank of brine and fish flesh left to rot.

Eric tapped at his phone. A moment later, a message chimed. "We're clear."

They watched in silence as he pulled out his video camera and began rolling.

"Now what?" Natalie asked.

"Now we take pictures of Eric as he shoots. Lots of pictures. From every angle. And then we all take pictures of each other taking pictures."

Natalie gave a little laugh. "Oh, that's clever. Then no one can say it's fake."

The mission didn't take long. They double-checked their camera rolls and then left. When they were back home, Peter busted out a bottle of port from a cupboard and poured everyone a glass.

Chapter 49

62°

Yuki hadn't forgotten Peter's promise to try yoga. After he finished his coffee, she marched him to one of the empty back rooms and pointed at a blue mat on the floor.

At first, his body didn't want to cooperate with her instructions, and when he complained that he'd lost all flexibility after giving up surfing, she replied in that brisk way of hers.

"Then this is exactly why you should be doing this, Peter. We're not doing anything performative here. We're not doing this for social media. We're going to get you nice and bendy and help that back of yours."

He had managed to get bendy enough with Carla last night, but he wasn't about to mention that to Yuki. Still, he did see it as a sign of hope that his body hadn't completely abandoned him yet. Peter just hoped whatever flexibility he managed to acquire in his first yoga session with Yuki was enough to power him through cleaning up his condo. Carla had suggested he hire one of those water damage and restoration companies to do the work, but he wanted to spend the money on other things. Like furniture for the new house and a ring for Carla now that she'd said yes.

Ever practical, Carla said, "Just a gold band, and nothing fancy. I don't want to ruin it in the kitchen."

Yuki was a good teacher. And patient as she showed him how to breathe through the poses. He felt ridiculous and hoped Lucas or Eric didn't walk in. Eric lived in Monterey, so he'd stayed the night, and he had the day off since he worked weekends.

Peter and Carla had gone to bed, leaving the young people talking late into the night.

At the end of the yoga session, he didn't exactly feel like a new man, but he could see how, with time, he might recapture the shape he'd lost and hopefully get back on a surfboard.

It would also be nice if he didn't throw his back out reaching for the soap in the shower.

Natalie asked Yuki to accompany her to meet with Olivia's parents. Carla tried to intervene because Yuki was grieving too. But Yuki seemed glad of something positive to do. After breakfast, the two set out. Lucas talked Eric into helping him clear the junk out of the studio in the backyard, and when they walked to the truck in the driveway, their voices drifted over the high fence.

"Dark blue is a horrible color," Eric said. "It's too small. It'll be like living in a cave."

"So? You're not going to live here," Lucas quipped.

"What? I'm not allowed to visit?"

"Maybe," Lucas said grudgingly. "If you're nice."

Peter's hand stalled on the door handle, eyes flicking to Carla, who looked like she was trying not to laugh.

"Wait. Am I missing something? Are they…flirting?"

Carla rolled her eyes. "Wow. You are late to that party." She smirked all the way to the San Refugio Ocean Condominiums.

The streets were clear of barricades. The tent had disappeared from the beach and the creature with it. A few smaller research ships remained offshore, but the large one was gone, presumably back to the lab in Moss Landing.

"My DNA results aren't back yet," Carla said as Peter pulled into the skinny street behind the complex. "I texted Jessica. She said it might be on hold for a while because of that thing they found."

"What happened to it? Do they know?"

"No. It washed up dead. She said it showed signs of disease, mucous or something, so it was probably sick. She's hoping that's the case for all of them—and that they'd die before they had a chance to reproduce."

"We can only hope," he said dryly.

The small parking lot was empty, but there were signs people had been there. Someone had cleaned out Maggie's place. Peter recognized her sodden furniture stacked next to the dumpsters. He felt sad seeing her favorite pieces ruined and discarded. Peter wandered over to the pile, running a finger along the warped arms of her favorite chair.

Unbidden, an image flashed in his mind—Maggie thrashing in the water as a stinger pierced her body. He shook his head, rubbed his eyes, and turned his attention to the other disaster looming just to his left.

Up close, they could see the full extent of the damage to the San Refugio Pier. The sides seemed to pull away from each other. Planks dangled above the water, its mid-section gone. There was nothing to connect the two ends of the structure, except an expanse of drooping cables and pipes.

Carla sighed. "That's going to cost millions."

They had to step over yellow caution tape to enter the pathway. The windows of Maggie's condo were boarded up, as were the others. Peter dreaded what they would find when they got to his place.

Someone had cleared the driftwood and debris from the sidewalk.

As they rounded the corner to his place, Carla flinched. "Oh no."

The windows were busted out, and the front door was off its hinges. It looked like a monster had taken a battering ram to the place. Peter had experienced the powerful storm surge firsthand, so he wasn't surprised. Still, just looking at the mess made him feel exhausted, and he hadn't even lifted a shovel yet to begin mucking it out.

"Maybe we *should* call someone," he said, shoulders slumping.

Carla scrunched up her face, taking in the damage. "We're here. We might as well get started. Maybe it's not as bad as we think."

It was worse.

A pile of driftwood blocked the entryway. It was as high as his waist, and when they'd finished clearing it out, he was sweating. So was Carla. She'd thrown off her flannel shirt and was pulling seaweed out of the doorway, wearing a black tank top that revealed her toned arms.

"God this stuff stinks," she said, grimacing.

The living room looked like the contents had gone through a blender, then been topped with tree branches and seaweed, sprinkled with a layer of sand and dirt. Peter braced his core to avoid straining his back and began pushing things aside, clearing a path to the kitchen. The table sat upside down on the stove, legs in the air. A chair dangled half in, half out of the picture window.

"That wall is going to have to be replaced," Carla said. "It looks like wet cardboard."

Peter couldn't remember the details of his insurance policy, but he knew it was good. Hopefully, it would not only cover the repairs, but pay for upgrades so it would look like one of those modern cottages that sold for top dollar.

The back rooms of the condo had been spared the worst of the damage. The water had reached his bedroom and the back bathroom, and the wood floor would have to come up, but the mess of debris stopped at the midpoint of the hallway.

Carla had disappeared downstairs. Peter followed.

The cement steps were gritty with sand. Peter's brother had given him a hard time for replacing the old wooden staircase, but past floods had badly warped them, and he'd seen no point in doing anything but the most practical thing.

As he rounded the bend, he heard Carla sloshing around, muttering.

And then he saw why.

With no way for it to drain out, water filled the basement like a stinky, filthy swimming pool. Carla was halfway across the room, water up to her waist, headed toward the high shattered window.

With a yelp, she pitched sideways and fell into the water. Peter's heart pounded in his chest. He'd just reached the bottom stair, nearly tripping over the kettlebells he hadn't used in a year, when she came up, sputtering.

"I'm fine," she shouted. "I'm fine." Twigs stuck to her hair. "My foot rolled on a branch or something."

"What are you doing down here?"

"I'm going to start the sump pump. Get the place dried out."

He could have done that himself, but that was Carla. Peter watched as she made her way to the opposite wall. When she reached it, she stopped.

"Isn't this about where it is?"

"About two feet to your right," Peter said.

She plunged her hand into the murky water, mouth pursed in disgust, and came up holding a black plastic hose and a power cord. "Got it!"

The bottom of the window was chest-high, so it was just a matter of draping the hose over the windowsill. Peter watched her reach up, plug the cord into a socket high on the wall, and click on the switch. Water began to splash outside onto the pavement. He cheered.

"This water is disgusting." Clara began to wade toward him. "I can't wait to take a fucking shower."

Chuckling, he wagged a finger at her. "You have a filthy mouth."

"Take a shower with me if you really want to hear me talk dirty," she warned.

In a shallow alcove opposite the stairs, the water rippled. Something red and smooth broke through the debris, crested, and disappeared again.

Carla must have heard it too because she froze, eyes going wide.

It must have washed in through the open window and been trapped. Or hadn't wanted to leave. Because it was waiting.

Seven feet, maybe eight separated Peter from Carla. He hadn't seen a tentacle yet, but that didn't mean there wasn't one. The water churned, a dark shadow writhing just below the surface.

He held his hand in the air in a silent plea for her to stay still. No sound, no movement. With the water so filled with debris, he could only hope it couldn't see her. The water rippled again, this time closer to Carla. Her shoulders had come up, and he could see the whites of her eyes. He couldn't remember her ever looking so frightened.

What happened next was a blur of motion.

A misshapen, bulbous black head rose out of the water. It swiveled on a thick, meaty stalk of a neck, the nictitating membrane blinking slowly. It paused as if in recognition. Its small mouth opened, widening as it unhitched its jaw and revealed two rows of jagged teeth.

But there was something wrong with its head. A thick, viscous slime coated its skin.

Carla stared at it, transfixed by its grotesque appearance, mouth slightly open.

And then it was slicing through the water toward her, and Peter was moving too, grabbing the first thing his hand could find—fingers wrapping around a kettle bell.

Carla threw herself to the side, her shoulder slamming against a wall.

The creature lunged out of the water, exposing its torpedo-shaped body, a shiny, sickening shade of red. Then Peter was swinging the kettle bell, the iron crashing against the creature's head. There was a sickening, meaty thud. He struck it again just before it vanished into the murky water.

Peter dragged Carla toward the stairs, still clutching the kettlebell, the weight of it tugging at his shoulder. But he wasn't about to let it go. Not until they were outside, standing on dry pavement, as far away from the water as they could get.

Just as they'd reached the bottom step, he turned around and saw a tentacle shoot out of the water. It flicked past him toward Carla, mucous-covered stinger quivering madly. He swung the kettle bell again, striking the tentacle so hard it and the weight broke through the wall, the momentum dragging Peter with it.

He released his hold on the handle and yanked his hand out of the hole in the wall. The tentacle twitched several times, then went still.

"Fuck this shit," Carla snarled.

She shoved past him and grabbed the second kettle bell. He had to flatten himself against the stairwell to avoid getting hit. Carla aimed at the thickest part of the tentacle and brought it down. Viscous fluid oozed out from rings surrounding the stinger.

They scrambled up the stairs, panting, and collapsed on the landing. She looked around, frantic, then gave a little cry of relief when she spotted her phone sitting on top of the railing.

She snapped a few pictures of the tentacle, then handed the phone to Peter. "Take a few of me with that in the background. Just in case."

When he was done, he stood and hauled her to her feet. For such a strong woman, she was surprisingly light.

Outside, the sun was breaking through the clouds. He could feel its weak warmth on the top of his head. They sat in his truck for a while, staring at the pier in numb silence, windows rolled down to let in the cool breeze. Carla sent the photos to Jessica Chen along with Peter's address so she could come collect the beast.

Their clothes were still wet. Water dripped on the seats.

Peter listened to the crashing surf. A flock of pelicans soared over the ruined pier.

He gripped the steering wheel. "I think that one was sick," he finally said.

Carla turned to him, eyes red. "Do you think that was Jacob?" she whispered. "It's eyes. They were brown."

He shook his head with more certainty than he felt. "No. That wasn't Jacob."

"I guess the DNA will tell us." She stared straight ahead.

Not if he could help it. Not if he got to Jessica Chen first.

"That wasn't Jacob," he repeated firmly. "Let's go home."

She sniffed, then rested her hand on his knee and stared out the window as they drove into the hills.

They rounded a corner, and the sun-faded, wind-battered yellow Victorian came into view. He felt like he was going home for the first time. To a real home, with people who felt like family.

While Carla took a long shower, Peter called Jessica Chen. She listened as he asked her to keep the results of her DNA study private.

"She does not need to know if that thing we killed had some of her son's DNA. It'll haunt her forever."

Jessica was silent for so long, Peter thought the connection had dropped.

Finally, a long sigh drifted through the tiny speaker. "Well, for reasons I won't go into, we're unable to extract the information necessary to make that determination. I'll explain that to Carla." She hesitated. "I don't think she'll believe me, though."

"You're wrong there. I think she'll be relieved."

"I hope so. And Peter, thank you for keeping my son safe through all of this. You, Carla, and Yuki."

"And Lucas."

Jessica sounded surprised. "And Lucas."

When they hung up, he checked on Carla. The shower was still running. He changed into dry clothes, went downstairs, and stepped through the French doors. It was breezy, the sun peeking through the clouds. They'd left the telescope outside. He wiped the eyepiece and peered through the viewfinder.

The mud had cleared from the ocean off San Refugio Beach. The waves sparkled enticingly in the sun.

From the bandshell, four small figures in wet suits appeared carrying surfboards. They paused briefly in front of the sign that said, "Beach Closed," then raced for the waves.

The End

Author's Note

If you're scratching your head wondering why you've never heard of San Refugio, I will save you the trouble of searching for it online.

It's a fictitious town that looks awfully like my hometown of Capitola on the central coast of California. Now, that's a name you may recall from January 2023 news headlines. A massive storm slammed into the village, destroying the pier and flooding restaurants along a street called The Esplanade.

We don't live in the village, but my husband and I walk there nearly every day. The morning after the big storm, we were shocked to see waves lapping the buildings and pounding the pier. And yes, the surf pushed up floorboards in several restaurants.

The San Refugio Beach Condos are based on the wildly colorful Capitola Venetian Condos. They sit alongside Soquel Creek just a few yards from the surf.

For weeks, every time we walked down Cliff Drive into the village, my mind went into overdrive. What if the storm surge washed in more than just debris? Since I love creature features, I began to imagine what sorts of creepy things those might be. You get the drift.

While the storm surge in this story is inspired by the storm that struck Capitola, I took liberties with the layout of the village.

Capitola is one of the oldest vacation areas on the Pacific Coast. If you haven't visited, you should! It's ridiculously charming. If you do, and if the weather is nice and the hour is right, chances are you'll find my husband and me lounging in green plastic chairs at the back of rebuilt Zelda's on the Beach, having a drink and staring at the beautiful and mostly peaceful Monterey Bay.

Keep Reading for a Preview of

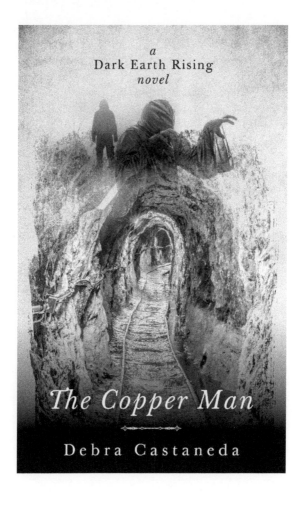

a
Dark Earth Rising
novel

The Copper Man

Debra Castaneda

Some grudges never die.

Chapter 1

George Cunliffe teetered on the edge of the Lower Prestwich Bridge, his back to the yawning open-pit mine and everything that had made his life a misery.

What he did not feel was guilt. What he had done, he would do again.

He could not remember the drive to the mine, where he had left his truck with the evidence inside, or how he'd come to choose this spot to end his life.

Oblivious to the icy wind against his face, he stared down at the enormous tailings pond, the liquid a reddish orange on one side, running to a sickly yellowish green on the other.

The wind pushed the hood of his jacket from his head. Wooden floor beams of the old trestle bridge groaned beneath his feet.

Time to get going.

His hands were stiff but steady as he tested the strength of the vertical post closest to him and found it solid. After looping the old, frayed rope around the base of the iron shaft, he tied a knot, then slipped the noose around his neck. He'd intended to get right to it—leap into the air, arms spread wide, welcoming death—but he found he wanted to prolong his time on the bridge, just a little. Long enough to remember the one good, beautiful thing in his pathetic life that had brought him joy.

He picked up a small rock from the railbed and scratched words into the rusted track. When he was done, he tossed the rock into the tailings pond and admired his work.

I CURSE THIS PLACE.

Lowering himself onto the rail ties, he swung his legs over the side, one hand gripping a diagonal brace. He kicked off his boots and flicked the rope behind his neck, as if it were a scarf getting in his way. Then, before he could think about another thing, he pushed himself off.

A scream escaped his lips.

He hadn't meant to scream. The noise ended abruptly, and for one long moment, pain seared his neck as the rope tightened. His hands flew up to the noose, fingers clawing at the fibers, and then he was falling.

His body slammed into the pond's sludgy, sucking bank.

He lay there for how long?

Seconds? Minutes?

The rope had snapped, that much he understood. Even though death was not instantaneous, it was surely just a matter of minutes. His insides had to be smashed to bits. His mouth tasted like blood and metal. He stared up at the sky, the clouds turning a murky and sinister orange.

Or was the copper color of the water altering his vision?

Rain drops hit his face, sharp and distinct. By some miracle, he was still alive, standing. Floating above the tailings pond. He gazed down at his still body in wonder.

Transformed. That's what he was. His thoughts came in flashes. Images. Thinking in this strange new language.

His old life was over. His mind—the one that had been attached to his broken body—had carried over into this new, strange existence he'd yet to explore. It was like a warm yellow glow coming from under a door. He yearned to push it open and see what was there. Or *who* was there.

"Son?" he cried.

Instead, he heard the distant shouting of men and felt the wetness of rain falling upon his face. Then all was dark, except his mind.

More Books by Debra Castaneda

Dark Earth Rising
Themed novels that can be read in any order

The Spore Queen
A charming reporter, an ailing tech mogul, and two strangers hiding secrets are brought together by a mysterious fungus, one that will either save them or destroy them.

The Devil's Shallows
Eight miles of mystery. One night of terror. Residents trapped in a remote neighborhood confront the unimaginable.

The Copper Man
Haunted tunnels. Unexplained deaths. Eerie sightings. Decades after The Copper Man killed her brother, Leah Shaw returns to the remote mining town of Tribulation Gulch where a lethal mystery awaits.

The Root Witch
A beautiful forest. A terrifying legend. It's 1986. Two strangers, hundreds of miles apart, grapple with disturbing incidents in a one-of-a-kind quaking aspen forest.

Circus at Devil's Landing

Creatures that howl in the night, a mysterious circus, and a clash between a ringmaster and a woman determined to rescue her captured lover.

Chavez Ravine Novels

Stand-alone novels set in Chavez Ravine, Los Angeles during turbulent times

The Monsters of Chavez Ravine

A 2021 International Latino Book Awards Gold Medal Winner! Before Dodger Stadium, dark forces terrorized Chavez Ravine.

The Night Lady

A rebel curandera, a plucky seamstress, and a young reporter are pulled into the investigation of a killer terrorizing Chavez Ravine.

www.ingramcontent.com/pod-product-compliance
Ingram Content Group UK Ltd.
Pitfield, Milton Keynes, MK11 3LW, UK
UKHW040123260225
4759UKWH00003B/151